Queen of the Waves

Lisa M. Bossier

Copyright © 2010 by Lisa M. Bossier

All rights reserved. No part of this book may be reproduced in any form or by any electronic or mechanical means, including information storage and retrieval systems, without written permission from the publisher, except by a reviewer who may quote brief passages in a review.

First Edition: May 2012

ISBN-13:978-1475101751

Printed in the United States of America

For My Beloved....

*For all who perished
And for all who survived
The storm of 1900*

*For those who bravely
Defended the U.S. Gulf Coast
During World War II*

*May your courageous
Legacy never be forgotten*

In dedication to

Sister Camillus Tracy

Sister Evangelist O'Sullivan

Sister Mary Elizabeth Ryan

Sister Mary Vincent Cottier

Sister Genevieve Davalos

Sister Mary Catherine Hebert

Sister Raphael Elliot

Sister Felicitas Rosner

Sister Benignus Doran

Sister Mary Finbar Creadon

and the children of St. Mary's Orphanage

who perished in the Great Storm of 1900

A special dedication and thank you to the late Michael W. Clayton, Sr., who, before passing away, shared accounts of the Great Storm of 1900 from the perspective of his grandfather, Nicholas J. Clayton.

Queen of the Waves

Chapter One

The sun blazed in the humidly warm afternoon sky, as the tide rose and fell in its usual repetitive measure. Beachcombers spent the day sunning themselves and splashing in the water along the shore's edge. Independence Day in Galveston was always marked with special celebrations, but this holiday was even more precious. It was 1900, and the dawning of a new century. The city was draped in red, white, and blue bunting. Festive banners and American flags flapped in the tropical breeze from gingerbread trimmed front porches. Acting as beacons for those out-of-towners feeling melted and weary, the Victorian rooftops gleamed with grandeur in the midsummer's heat, beckoning all to come to the seashore and rest their sweaty brows. Sea gulls bobbed up and down like kites above the beachcombers, eagerly awaiting crumbs of food. The gulls' loud, mischievous cackling added to the joyful melody of the waves while a squadron of pelicans patrolled the tepid horizon.

While families celebrated the holiday afternoon together, the children of St. Mary's Orphanage romped and laughed on the beach savoring slices of watermelon and indulging in spoonfuls of vanilla ice cream that a cherished benefactor provided as a surprise treat. The patriotic chandeliers that cascaded through the night sky marked the last celebration Galveston, Texas would enjoy for quite awhile. Unimaginably, there was a monster preparing to rise out of the Gulf that would bring calamitous ruin to thousands.

Chapter Two

"What is the lesson Shakespeare seeks to get across in *Hamlet?* We just read *Richard III* a few weeks ago, so what is Shakespeare trying to say about politics, royalty, and family? What do these lessons say to our society right now, as our country is in the midst of a war?"

Marie grew frustrated as she realized that only two out of the twenty-five kids in her class were listening to her. The rest were intently watching a ghost-like fog encroach over the schoolyard.

"Does anyone have an answer for me?"

"Mrs. Covington, it's Friday afternoon, it's July, and those are stories of long ago. Why should we care? It's boring. It doesn't have anything to do with history or even what's happening now. These are just stories."

Though the class would only be in session for a few weeks of the summer, Marie was keenly aware that Bobby Biltz's apathy was a highly contagious disease that required immediate containment. These were privileged students who were extremely talented and were blessed enough to come from households that could afford their children the best educational experiences money could buy so soon after the Depression. At this time, money still was very tight for most everyone. Marie worried a great deal about the stresses the world's situation was placing on her students in her class and how their reaction to educational excellence was to simply shut down and be apathetic. Marie believed her students cared about their education more than they could show. She knew they were emotionally exhausted by all that was going on around them. A hub for the Navy and Marines, Galveston was full each week of goodbyes and sad reunions as military men were either deploying to various destinations in Europe and the Pacific or being returned home in wooden coffins on the noon train. The disruptions Galvestonians continually faced in their daily lives were constant reminders of a real war with real risks. The regular siren drills, Navy air patrols, and the strict lights out curfew at dusk every evening helped to fuel wartime anxieties. Each time an air raid siren sounded or the air patrol flew over, Marie cringed as the sounds caused her to remember a year ago when a German submarine was spotted roughly two hundred miles offshore from Galveston. The sighting triggered

Queen of the Waves

a direct war time order for all Texas coastal cities to turn out all lights for several days. Anyone caught violating this edict with lights on after seven in the evening faced being charged with wartime crimes and possible charges of treason. This first complete blackout in U. S. history left a traumatic impact on Marie. The increasing reports of German U-boat sightings off the coasts of Texas and Louisiana only added more fuel to the fears she and others harbored. The perpetual apprehension of a German invasion of U-boats upon Galveston, as well as other coastal cities along the Gulf, was a quiet phantom that preyed upon even the calmest person's nerves, but especially in the minds of imaginative children. Marie understood quite well that her students were overwhelmed. World War II was in full bloom. In the midst of war, no one nonmilitary would want to study war, especially when their fathers, uncles, brothers, and cousins were overseas fighting. Even Marie's concentration was jilted, as her beloved husband, Charlie, was in France fighting in the war. In fact, Marie's greatest fear was in having an officer appear on her doorstep to deliver the news that her Beloved had been killed. Each day, she managed to squash this fear into the furthermost point in her mind, but every now and then the fear resurfaced like a large rogue wave, temporarily washing away the confident foundation that rooted her.

Queen of the Waves

"Bobby, I appreciate your opinion of Shakespeare and I am disappointed you feel this way. However, as long as each of you is attending class in my classroom, you will all dig deep and find a reason to care about literature and history. The events and discoveries that happened either long ago or just yesterday continue to shape us today and leave an impression on the future. I'll share with you a little secret. The dates are significant only in the placement of time. What is important are the people, the influences around them, their motivations, and the ramifications of those motivations. These are the things that shape our world and are crucial to our understanding of how we arrived to where we are today. Within every story, the author intends to express a thesis, a central universal point to the audience. Now, since the bell is about to ring, over the weekend, I want you to write an essay answering the question I wrote on the board earlier. What is the central message Shakespeare hopes to convey to his audience in *Hamlet* and *Richard III*?"

As the bell rang, the students leapt towards the door. Worried that she still wasn't heard, Marie hollered after them. "Don't forget—I want your essays first thing Monday. Have a good weekend."

Queen of the Waves

As the last student exited the doorway, Marie leaned against her desk and pinched the top of her nose, as she always did when she's stressed and frustrated. She took a deep sigh and walked around to her desk chair to resume grading exams from her morning classes. "I'm so thankful it is Friday," thought Marie.

Collecting her papers, Marie looked out the large arching window that overlooked the schoolyard. Transfixed by the heavy, misty fog, she walked over to the window to look further. She liked when a freak cool front would sneak a surprise appearance in July, when the warm Gulf breeze became overrun with cool Canadian air. For the island, this equation always created a blanket of intense fog. The fog, to many Galvestonians, was a morose sight. To Marie, it helped her cope with the melancholy in her heart. It was days like this one that made her feel that if nature could hide itself until it knew what season it was in, then she could do the same. As it was for all Americans, these were deeply troubled times that she, her husband, and her students were facing.

Marie drew the blinds and decided it was time to go home for the weekend. She grabbed her brown leather satchel off her desk. Reaching for the light switch while reflecting to just moments earlier with her class, she hoped her students

Queen of the Waves

would realize how literature is a reflection of history and history's impact on society.

The route home was the usual. She enjoyed the mysticism of her walk. Having lived in Galveston a few years, Marie had seen many foggy days, but today's fog seemed much heavier than her recent memory could serve. Walking down Broadway, Marie approached Old Main Cemetery. Reveling in the eeriness of the moment, she decided to take a walk through the cemetery. She always meant to walk through and survey the markers of those buried in the historic cemetery, and today was going to be that day.

Ivory colored statues graying with age faded into the foggy air. The white opaqueness was tinged with the heavy scent of sea air and oleanders. At times, the breeze was cool; but, just when your skin felt the coolness refreshing, the air changed to a whisper of warm Gulf air. With each step, a statue emerged from the shroud of whiteness. Many tombstones were dated 1898. Marie pondered what happened in 1898 to cause so many deaths. A beautiful tombstone with a marble angel caught Marie's eye. She gazed at the masterful craftsmanship of the statue. Infant 2 was the name on the grave. This saddened Marie. "How could someone be born into this world and pass through without being given a name?" she questioned out loud to herself. Seeking further solitude, Marie slowly walked to the edge of the cemetery and sat on a marble bench. She admired the dramatic contrast of the pink blossoming oleanders against the dreary monochromatic backdrop. The oleanders grew to create a five-foot wall of green stems, leaves, and white and pink blossoms. Their fragrance was quite pungent with its sweet and intoxicating smell. Marie admired the tall thick plants, especially the pink blossoms. She picked a pink blossom and placed it behind her ear in her long brown hair. While selecting a blossom to pick, she came to the amazing realization that the oleanders were growing through a rather sturdy yet rusty iron fence. Intrigued, Marie tried to separate the oleanders to find more of the fence. Marie pushed and pushed to separate the oleanders, but they were too thick and too heavy for her to move. Frustrated and tired, Marie resolved that she would return tomorrow to further explore the iron fence.

Daylight could not break soon enough for Marie. Before the dawn's first light, Marie returned to the cemetery for further exploration. The headstones and markers began to gleam a ghostly white pallor, as the night sky gave way to sullen lavender. Cautiously, she made her way through the historic cemetery towards the oleanders concealing the iron fence. A soft breeze moved the oleanders along the fence in a rhythmic lull. It was a cool, clammy, misty morning. Spade in hand, Marie pushed aside the overgrown weeds and oleanders. Straining, she pulled herself onto and then over the fence. One leg at a time, she crossed over into the mysteriously hidden part of the cemetery. Weeds and grass had overgrown so wildly that markers and tombstones were barely visible. Without a moment's thought, Marie knew she needed to cleanup these overgrown graves.

Finally clearing the horizon, the sun remained hidden behind a heavy shroud of clouds. Oddness was in the air, but Marie attributed the feeling to being in a cemetery. Looking down at the weeds and overgrowth at her feet and then around her in the strangely segregated area, she was intrigued with why this area was sectioned off and questioned internally how long it would take her to clear away the overgrowth to reveal just one marker. She slowly took a few steps forward, feeling the corner of something hard with her right foot. Marie instantly knelt down to find that clover and roots had grown across a marker. With her spade, she began to dig away the roots, grass, and weeds. More of the marker's face emerged with each swipe. Marie worked faster and faster with curious excitement. As if seeing an apparition, Marie marveled at the

Queen of the Waves

image on the marker. Engraved on gray marble was a beautifully carved image of the Holy Mother and the name of Sister Mary Vincent Cottier. Marie slowly moved her hand across the dirty tombstone as though she was reading braille. She was moved by how this poor woman had been forgotten in time with so much overgrowth on her gravesite.

Without realizing, time passed in hurried measure; Marie was so consumed with care and concern over the buried markers that she barely stopped to take a rest. Five graves had been uncovered and to Marie it was as though she was on a historic treasure hunt. Her curiosity was greatly aroused. She queried why all of these graves were grouped together, how they died, and why they passed away on September 8, 1900. She wondered even more about a grave labeled with just the name Susie Fenton that looked the size of a child's grave. Even more engrossed, Marie clawed at the earthy growth to reveal yet another marker. Ruby Mae Bastrop was the name on the tombstone, with the dates August 10, 1894–September 8, 1900 inscribed. She was moved to tears as she became even more aware that a tragic story was slowly revealing itself to her.

Suddenly, there was a loud creek and heavy steps. Marie looked up in time to see the oleanders along the old fence move, signaling someone was there. A high-pitched metallic squeak clanged as the gate for the rusted iron fence moved inward. Marie's heart rate jumped as a tall lanky figure emerged from the green rustic barrier. The shadowy image of a man stood before her. Raspily, the man charged, "What are you doing here? This place is sacred. Leave at once!"

Slowly, the figure approached her, and she glimpsed a facial image. The lanky man standing before her was roughly seventy years old. He had long, matted grayish blonde hair that fell just below his waist, and a weathered face that was somewhat hidden beneath a gray scraggily beard.

"Leave here at once!"

Tinged with fear, Marie shakily stood up. Dusting off her long black skirt, she apologized and grabbed her basket containing a spade, gloves, and some other gardening items.

"I'm sorry. I really didn't mean any harm. I came through here yesterday and thought it sad that these graves are all overgrown. I thought they needed a little love and care; so, I came back to clear them off and make them pretty."

Marie carefully walked towards the hidden gate.

"Wait ma'am. I misunderstood your intentions. Please continue. It is okay if you stay," said the stranger in a crisply guarded tone.

Queen of the Waves

Shaken by the initial fierceness of his voice and his overbearing presence, Marie's mind locked temporarily and all she could do was stand frozen for a few minutes before carefully walking back to where she was pulling up weeds. She kept her brown eyes fixed on the stranger as she knelt down by the grave, feeling very unsure of him. Marie studied all of his features and began making impressions about him and his life. He stood tall, roughly six feet and five inches. She assumed his severely weathered face meant that he was once a fisherman or someone accustomed to hard work in the sun. His clothes were incredibly worn, as if they had not been changed in over a year. She even wondered when he last bathed. As crystal blue as a shimmering oasis, Marie was stirred by his eyes and how they held a secret gentleness. Though they reminded her a bit of her Charlie's eyes, these eyes seemed deeply sad. Perhaps, this man was a lost soul who had once loved and lived passionately, but something dramatic happened that lead him to his current state. By looking into those eyes, she knew there was a story residing inside of him. Camouflaged by his voice and appearance, Marie chose to believe he was a gentle giant who had been suffering desperately of loneliness for quite some time.

Marie quickly tried to break the silence and awkwardness between them. She stood, dusted off her skirt again, took a few steps toward him, and, extending her hand to him with a nervous smile, said, "I am Marie."

The mysterious figure suspiciously studied her and then hesitantly extended his hand to her. Expressionless, he gave her a brief nod. Then, in a sudden movement, he grabbed hold of the gold crucifix charm on Marie's necklace. In a softer, but still scratchy voice remarked, "Does this imply that you are a Catholic?"

Shaken by the man's abrupt actions and concerned that his hand was too close to her neck while not knowing his intentions, Marie answered the only answer she could say.

"I am."

The man held onto the crucifix a little longer and his face morphed from complete sternness into an almost weepy expression of relief.

"Well, then maybe it's really okay for you to be here."

Perplexed as to why he did not give her his name, she went back to the area she was weeding. Slowly, Marie resumed her digging and pulling up weeds, but she kept him fixed in the corner of her eye. He sat down next to the fence and, without

Queen of the Waves

saying a word, watched her work. The presence of this stranger and the odd silence weighed on Marie's nerves.

"I should be going," Marie said nervously.

"No, please, do not let my being here interrupt the good work you are doing," spoke the strange man with an almost pleading emphasis.

As she does when she's nervous, Marie proceeded with idle conversation, though it completely was one-sided. She talked about her husband and how they moved to Galveston from St. Louis. She prattled on about her love of literature, William Shakespeare, and her students. Hours and hours passed and still only Marie was talking. The stranger just sat and listened expressionless. Marie continued and pondered out loud what she was going to do with Bobby Biltz. She discussed her worries about the war. She gushed proudly of how much she adores her husband, Charlie. Marie didn't realize that, while she was nervously prattling on and on, the stranger was listening rather intently on all she had to say.

In the midst of her talking, the thought struck Marie that perhaps she should not be so conversational with this stranger. After all, she was alone and this remembrance made her feel vulnerable all of a sudden. She decided to turn the tables and see if she could get this stranger to start talking a bit.

Wiping her dirty gloves and beaded brow, Marie reached for her lunch pail.

"Would you like half of my sandwich?"

Marie gladly shared half her sandwich with the quiet man.

"May I ask your name?"

"My name is Woodrow, but those who really know me call me Woody. It's mighty nice of you to be going through all of this effort. I'm sure if they could tell you, they would tell you how much they appreciate it too."

"It's just such a pity for all of this to be so overgrown. Besides, I need a diversion from my current reality."

"And what reality is that?"

Marie choked back an onslaught of emotions by looking downward, furrowing her brow, and biting her bottom lip. Her voice crackled each time she started to speak. Finally, she again found her voice.

"That this world is falling apart at the seams and I'm terrified I may never again see my husband alive. When he was leaving, he told me he knew I could handle all of this because he thinks I am a strong person. I don't know what lead him to believe that about me. Each day I don't hear from him, I fall apart inside a little more."

Queen of the Waves

Woody felt great empathy for Marie. He understood well the feelings of fear and loss. He, too, once danced a fully daunting dance card with despair and uncertainty. Though he did not say much, he found her company enchanting.

"How long has it been since you last heard from your husband?"

"It has been two months and three days. You know, I've had plenty of silence to think since Charlie has been gone. I think into everyone's life, at some moment, comes a living hell. For some, it may be temporary, while others remain stuck in a perpetual place of doom. This hell can present itself in various places, persons, or situations. I believe deeply that it is these flashes of hell that have the power to make people stronger and grow closer to God. Others, however, go the opposite way, become resentful, and turn their backs against God and His goodness. I'm facing that hell right now. I'm desperately trying to see God's face in the midst of all this going on around me. I'm struggling to feel God's love when the greatest love of my life has been ripped away from me and may never return to me, and this beautiful country may be taken and lost in the war."

The passionate surge of emotional pain caught Marie off guard and she was quite astounded with all that she had just revealed to a complete stranger. Working to restrain herself from crying, Marie was caught up in all the raw emotions that were building inside of her. She pondered the torment of her heart and queried whether she would be strong enough to overcome all of the darkness that played before her every day. Marie also wondered about her students and the hellish struggles they were all enduring. Suddenly, Marie's tone was serenaded by the sound of shrill air raid sirens. Marie looked up at the sky and glanced around, wiping a few tears that managed to slip from her eyelids. The deafening sound reinforced the hellish lost and empty feelings inside of her. Trusting the sirens were only another drill, Marie glanced at Woody across the way and then resumed pulling up weeds and grass.

Woody lowered his head a bit, as if in a moment of solemn reflection. "Keep the faith that your husband is fine and living for you just as you are living for him. Love…it will keep you going and give you strength you didn't know you had. You hold onto that love for that husband of yours. Love is what saved my life and keeps me hanging on each day. It is what saved me from that hell you just mentioned."

"Thanks for your supportive words," said Marie, as she gathered her things, ready to head home. She was still quite misty eyed, and felt overwhelmed by all of the emotions that had resurrected from deep within her heart. As Marie walked home, she mulled over what Woody had said to her. Woody's words touched her. She wondered what life lessons had caused him to speak with such unsuspecting heart. Upon Marie's arrival home, she stood at her gate and marveled at the way the sun's light played upon her house. She admired the way the light blue color of her two-story Victorian home glowed. Even the white gingerbread that lined the house and front porch looked so vibrant in the late afternoon sun. The sun's casting of unusual radiance lifted Marie's spirits and gave her a new surge of energy, though she could not quite grasp why her spirits felt so lifted because the lighting looked so pretty. While still staring at her illuminated home, Marie opened the mailbox outside the front gate. She was overjoyed to find a letter from her Charlie waiting for her. With great glee, she snatched the letter out of the box. She ran through the gate and up the porch steps where she dropped to sit on the top step to read it. Marie's heart skipped with excited anticipation, and she questioned the coincidence of the unusual radiance upon the house while, at the same time, there was news from her Beloved. Carefully, she opened the envelope and lovingly pulled out the contained letter.

Queen of the Waves

Darling Marie,

I'm on guard tonight and tomorrow. I've just come off my turn of duty and it's now a little after 8 p.m. I admit I'm quite sad and lonely. Do not feel too sorry for me. I realize you are probably feeling pretty blue yourself, but I need you to remember how proud I am of you. I need you to be the strong lady that you are. I'm sorry I've been skimpy on the letters as of late. Would have liked to have gotten a letter to you sooner, but we're all kept busy. Things have been pretty ugly here. Got the gift box you sent me. It was swell. I really appreciate the cookies, the Bible, and the picture of you. I've been keeping the picture of you close to me at all times. My, how I wish I were home with you. The picture made me think of how I miss our nights in the gazebo laughing and talking until the moon got too tired to stand watch over us. How I miss you and being able to look into your eyes! Please continue the prayers for me. The perfume on your letters is a very nice touch and makes me picture you even more. Your loving words fuel my waning spirit. I often fall asleep in the embrace of your warm words. When I get home I'm going to build you that arbor you have been wanting; and to grow across it, we can plant those roses you like. I so deeply long to be home with you. I love you and miss you more than you would ever believe.

Forever Yours,
Charlie

Marie read and reread the letter several times. She held it close to her. By doing so, she hoped he could feel her warm embrace and she could feel his embrace in return. Tears of joy, concern, anxiety, loneliness, fatigue, and sheer love ran down

Queen of the Waves

Marie's face. She gently pulled the letter to her nose to see if she could detect the slightest resemblance of his scent. She could not, but she could clearly see him in her mind—his tall slim stature, the broad shoulders, dirty blonde hair, those dazzling blue eyes, and that warm smile he always wore beneath a blonde mustache. Marie prayed with every ounce of her being that there soon would be a day where he'd be walking up the front walk and she'd be running down the porch steps to welcome home her precious hero. Charles Francis Covington—she loved this man so deeply and desperately wanted him home with her. The pain she felt in missing him was excruciating.

A natural optimist, Charlie was an honorable and intelligent man who was slow to anger and quick to forgive. The second he first saw Marie at a church picnic in the summer of 1938 on the St. Louis banks of the Mississippi River, he knew he'd love her for the rest of his life. Upon first sight of Marie, he was enraptured with her grace and the simple sweet quiet manner she kept. He loved the mystery of her smile, and the gentleness of her brown eyes. The way her lacy pink, white, and lavender floral dress fluttered in the breeze captivated him; he thought she looked like an angel. He longed to be a part of her quiet abode—for he could tell she'd be kind to his heart, and he instantly felt that he could trust her with his life. Charlie lovingly made Marie his bride on June 2, 1939. A savvy banker, he moved Marie to Galveston in 1940 to seek out textile business ventures on the Texas Gulf Coast. He managed to build a nice and comfortable life for the two of them. While war began to build and rage in Europe, Charlie took comfort in knowing that for a good while his beloved Marie would be sheltered from the financial worries that were afflicting many Americans. Where he found great pride in providing her with all of the comforts and securities of life, Marie found great pride and joy in not only feeding his stomach, but in keeping his heart and soul fed as well. Devout Catholics, the foundation of their marriage was in witnessing and living their faith together. They longed for the day when they would have children. However, this would not be happening any time soon, as Charlie was drafted into the Army.

While he was concerned for her welfare while he was away at war, Charlie believed Marie to be a strong woman. She thought herself to be more of a dutiful problem solver than strong. She also rebuked being called strong because she thought it sounded too masculine. The oldest of six children, Marie found herself in the difficult position of losing her parents, two sisters, and a brother to an influenza outbreak when she was just fourteen. The tragic family loss catapulted her into the role of caregiver of her two younger sisters who were only six and eight years old. While Marie stubbornly did her best to look after and raise her sisters on her own, she finally surrendered and agreed for her Aunt Mavis and Uncle Pete to take them into their home. It was that hand of fate that lead directly for Marie to cross paths with Charlie. If she had not surrendered, then Marie would not have been attending St. John's Catholic Church and would not have been at that fateful church picnic where she was introduced to Charles Covington.

Marie longed for Charlie's arms. She knew very well the torture of loss and isolation. Though distant memories, flashbacks of when she was barely a teenage girl were there to remind her of what it was like to be scared of the future, while the weight of responsibilities and hardships were bearing down, causing her to question if true happiness could ever really find her. For all she had endured in her early life, she believed that Charlie was God's gift of joy to compensate her for all of the sadness and pain, and to remind her that there is a season for everything in life. In the second she met Charlie, Marie felt her dark skies part to make way for this blonde and enthusiastic light that would consume her heart.

Queen of the Waves

Returning to her senses, Marie rose from the top step and walked inside their home, blotting the tears streaming down her face with the back of her right hand. She walked upstairs to her bedroom to take further comfort there. Her bedroom was small and simple, as the house was constructed at the turn of the twentieth century. The walls were beige with white baseboards that went around the room. Marie loved the window. The window had two panels of glass that came together to make one large window roughly five feet across. Gold drapes masked the outside world to keep the bedroom a safe haven. The room consisted of an elaborately carved oak bed, oak dressing table, a matching chest of drawers, and a tall intricately carved wardrobe. The dressing table was her favorite piece. She loved sitting in front of the mirror framed in tiger oak each evening to brush out her long brown hair after having it pinned up all day. Beautiful glass knobs adorned the doors to her closet and bedroom. Marie's bed, though beautiful, served as a constant reminder of her absent Charlie. A single cherry wood-framed chair stood in front of the window, as Marie loved to sit and watch the view of the ocean. Sitting in front of the window was another way to grasp a piece of serenity in the midst of so much horror happening in the world. She often sat in the chair and wondered what her Charlie was doing, if he was okay, when he had last eaten, if he was injured, when he would be coming home, and praying he had not been taken prisoner or gasped his last breath. Marie believed her Charlie was still alive because she earnestly believed that if he were gone—she would feel the life force within her grow weak. They were that close of a couple and so in sync that, though they were thousands of miles and an ocean away, they could feel each other's presence.

Placing the letter next to her on the bed, Marie stared at the elegant Swiss blue topaz and diamond wedding ring on her finger and how it sparkled in the sunlight shining through the window. Thoughts of Charlie at war made her utterly alone. She instead pondered more about the cemetery, all of the markers she had cleared off, and about the vague stranger, Woody. As she mulled over her day, she found herself again questioning how she could have revealed so much about herself to a complete stranger. She knew she was sad and felt miserable at times, but she didn't think she was that lonely.

Marie's life wasn't exactly a solitary one; she had her friends. There was Bootsie Miller, whose given name was Katherine. She was a twenty-year-old gorgeous brunette who lived with her family on Broadway, which, according to Galveston standards, was a sign of a wealthy pedigree. Bootsie was madly in love with Frank Carlson. However, the bloom of love between Bootsie and Frank was poisoned at times by the intervening ways of the reddish blonde Eugena Carlson, Frank's twin sister. Because of her perpetual verve and aggressiveness for life, Moxie was the nickname most everyone called Eugena. Moxie adored her brother, and saw Bootsie as a complete threat to her brother's attention. Fear of losing her brother motivated Moxie to thwart Frank's feelings for Bootsie in the most beguiling ways. Because Bootsie and Moxie were the same age and ran in the same social circles, it was easy for Moxie to know the details of Bootsie's day to day life. If another guy so much as glanced at Bootsie, Moxie would run immediately to Frank with a contrived tale of Bootsie having a new boyfriend or how Bootsie was a false goody-goody. The tragedy for Frank was in how much he trusted his sister. His trust lasted until the day he caught Moxie behind St. Patrick's one Sunday after Mass. He eavesdropped on Moxie and the tale she fed Bootsie of how he was in love with someone else and that Bootsie's family was too rich for the Carlson's blood. Frank at once broke up the cat fight and was overwhelmed with the joy in realizing that all along Bootsie did love him. He was also stunned to realize his sister's manipulative ways. Though Frank and Bootsie rejoiced from that day forward in their love for each other, being discovered did not stop Moxie from pulling more antics. This made things very difficult for Marie, as she was friends with both Moxie and Bootsie. Frank's being drafted by the Navy and sent out into the Pacific made things even more awkward for Marie, as the tensions between Bootsie and Moxie dramatically increased with Frank's departure. Frank's marriage proposal to Bootsie before shipping out sent Moxie reeling even further into the stratosphere. With Moxie fixated on the fear of losing her brother one way or another, and Bootsie functioning in a perpetual defensive mode, Marie soon found it was easier to distance herself from both Bootsie and Moxie because she found one always wanted to talk about the other. She understood clearly why Frank felt oddly glad to be shipping away from the war at home. Even for Marie, it was too much drama at one time. Instead, she preferred to retreat inside herself to gain a better grasp of her own concerns. Her neighbors also more or less kept to themselves. The exception was Mrs. Hillary Winthorpe, who was the bona fide neighborhood gossip. Mrs. Winthorpe was someone most untrustworthy because she shared every tidbit she knew as prime gossip at her neighborhood teas and luncheons. Other friends and acquaintances, like Stella McKellan and Freida

Schreiber were busy trying to hold their lives together while their husbands were off serving in the war. Many women, like Stella and Freida, rose at dawn each day to catch the bus to take them into Texas City to work in the factories all day only to return in the evening almost too tired to care for their families or even to socialize. Indeed, like Marie, many women were living lives of frenzied solitude.

As Marie reflected further, uncovering those hidden graves offered her a deep and fulfilling sense of satisfaction and a renewed sense of purpose. She planned to return to the cemetery after Mass tomorrow. Humming the popular tune *Somewhere Over the Rainbow*, she remained deep in thought while affectionately spinning her wedding ring on her finger. Marie also wondered if her students would have their themes ready for her Monday morning. With only one more week of summer school, she was more ready than her students to be done with classes. There was too much swirling around her to be able to focus on lesson plans.

July typically is a hot month in Galveston. The hot steamy air of late July, at times, can be quite sweltering and miserable. In fact, it sometimes can be downright overbearing. Despite the heat, Marie, with the help of Woody, worked hard to clean up the forgotten area. Though they were becoming friends, she felt a bit perplexed as to who this man was that came to visit her each day at the cemetery for the last couple of weeks. She figured he might be homeless and wondered about his past and if he had a family. Afraid to be perceived as nosy or a busybody, Marie remained polite in not asking too many questions—she just soaked up information when he provided it. Hesitant to admit it, Marie enjoyed Woody's company due to the loneliness she felt in the absence of her husband. She missed having someone to talk to regularly.

"It's going to be a hot one today," said Woody, as he stumbled through the gate, staggering from the heat and his age. "It seems there may be storms coming later. The birds are all acting funny."

"Are they?" replied Marie as she reached to pull up some more vines off a tombstone while studying the sky and trees for birds to denote odd behavior. "I do believe you are right about the heat today."

The freshly removed vines revealed the name Amelia Franco. Woody sat down under a tree for some shade. Upon seeing the unshrouded grave, he came to his feet, stumbled over, and then clumsily knelt down in front of the tombstone. With his back to Marie, he quietly made the Sign of the Cross and tenderly traced the surface of each letter with his right

Queen of the Waves

hand. Tears welled up in his eyes and he whispered, "It's been years since I've seen your name, but I've been right here everyday. You're still my Angel. I love you. I'm hoping I'll be joining you soon." Singular salty droplets seeped from Woody's tired eyes and streamed down his sundried face, as he leaned forward and kissed the warm stone marker.

"The roots to some of these weeds are just incredible. They're so strong—it's as though they could be used as rope to bind things together. Did you say something?"

Marie was oblivious to the emotional scene taking place behind her. She instead was distracted with getting as many gravesites as clean as possible. Woody wiped his eyes and face. He did not want Marie to see his tears.

"I was just whispering a prayer. That's what you do when you get to be my age. Them weeds are strong. You should take it easy or you'll cut your hands all up."

The morning passed quickly to the late afternoon. Marie stopped and wiped her brow, removed her straw hat, and held her forehead for awhile. "I'm going to have to be leaving and get some lunch. I'm just not feeling well. I'm feeling rather light-headed. I thought my breakfast would have lasted me a bit longer, but I need to go home."

"Well, I hope it's not sun stroke. Let me walk you home."

"No, thank you. I'm sure I'll be quite alright."

"Ma'am, I insist. You've been doing all of this work for several days and I appreciate it. Let me walk you to your gate."

Reluctantly, Marie accepted his offer in case she actually did pass out from the heat. Slowly, they strolled eastward down Broadway Street. Richardsonian-styled mansions constructed of rough-cut Texas granite intermixed with traditional pastel-colored clapboard Victorian-styled homes lining the main thoroughfare. Broadway was the street address for the most prominent Galvestonians, and the main street in the coastal town. The Covingtons were not among the most prominent, but they were able to live just a few blocks south of those that were. While her home wasn't one constructed of Texas granite, it was a fine and prominent home by its own right.

"I appreciate your walking me and not letting me be alone. My, it looks like clouds are moving in. Maybe a sea breeze rain will cool things down. You mentioned back at the cemetery that you appreciate my cleaning up those graves. Why…why do you appreciate it so? Do you know any of those people? Do they mean something to you?"

Woody was struck by the particularly personal questions that stirred deep emotions within him. The more he felt with his heart, the courser his voice became.

"I appreciate that you are restoring their identities. Their legacy has been forgotten by most. They all meant something. They were truly unforgettable people."

Marie wanted to uncover more on what it was exactly that Woody hasn't forgotten, but she was already at her gate on Avenue M. She thanked Woody again for the walk. Thinking it odd to invite him in, she asked him to wait while she made him a quick sandwich he could take with him. Returning to her kitchen, a sudden gust of wind caught Marie's attention. The sturdy magnolia tree in the backyard abruptly blew back and forth in a violent swishing motion. The image caused Marie to remember that last day Charlie was home. It was underneath the magnolia tree that they had a candlelit dinner and found themselves lost in the melody *Falling Leaves*. For a second, it all came back to her—the smell of the night's sea air infused with the sweet scent of magnolia blossoms, the loving way Charlie peered into her eyes, how safe she felt as they held each other beneath an exquisite full moon.

Marie groggily awoke feeling clammy. Her skin was a bit sweaty from the heavy humidity. To her astonishment, an entire day had passed in what seemed to be only minutes. She intended to only take a nap, but managed to sleep into the next morning. Rain wildly tapped on the windows. The pulsation of lightning caused the thunder to roar. As she awakened more from the foggy feeling inside her mind from sleeping so hard, a loud rhythmic booming noise caught her attention. Trying to understand why it was so dark for so early in the day, Marie hastened her way across the wood floor to the staircase and down the stairs just as the grandfather clock chimed nine o'clock. A booming noise continued to echo throughout the house. She soon realized that someone was knocking on her front door. As Marie made her way through the house to the door, she noted the torrential rain hitting her roof. The quick flicker of lightning lighted her way, though the sudden bolts striking nearby caused her to periodically flinch. The closer she got to the front door, the more frantic the visitor knocked.

"What on Earth?" mumbled Marie, as she peered through the window to see who was knocking so noisily and making such a commotion.

"My goodness!" Marie hurriedly opened the door. "Woody, what's the meaning of this? Thrashing on my door in the midst of a thunderstorm." Marie flinched at another sharp clap of thunder.

"Miss Marie, I've come to warn you. This is no ordinary thunderstorm! I've seen this before and you have cause to make haste with immediate preparations!"

"Come in out of the rain, Woody. What do you mean?"

"Miss Marie, if I know one thing, it's the look, smell, and taste of a hurricane. Let me help you fasten the storm shutters!"

As Woody spoke, Marie became aware that the wind was wickedly whipping things around outside. "Here—I'll fasten these window shutters. You shutter those."

She then went around the house gathering supplies and then placing them on the calico marble gaming table in the den. The house secured as best as it could be at such late notice, Marie and Woody sat in the living room, a room without any external walls. Having never experienced a storm as severe as this, Marie felt very nervous. She reached over to turn on the radio for news on the severe weather, and if it would be passing quickly through the area. She felt foolish for being so scared, and yet she could not help it all at the same time.

"Thanks for listening to WHAB, Galveston's local news provider. Currently, heavy thunderstorms are in the area, but they should be clearing out soon. Let us turn now to our field reporter, Steve Lawson, on news of the latest war developments."

To her astonishment, nothing notable was mentioned at all about the weather.

"Amazing. He didn't really say anything at all about how nasty it is outside. I've never seen wind like this. This is something more than just a heavy thunderstorm," said Marie while turning off the static-filled radio. Unexpectedly, Marie jumped in reaction to a sudden brilliant bolt of lightning that triggered a deafening clap of thunder and took out the power. The power gone, Marie lit a lantern and some candles to brighten the room for both of them.

"The storm sounds like it is getting worse."

"That's the nature of these monsters. It's only just now beginning," quipped Woody.

"Being from St. Louis, I've never been in a hurricane. From the sounds of it, it can be a bit frightful. Have you been through a hurricane before? You seem to have a bit of experience."

"I have. They are devastating monsters that crush dreams, tear loved ones apart, and leave behind a lifetime of heartache," responded Woody with a strong tone of bitterness.

"Where were you in one?" Marie asked carefully, noting the dissonant tone in Woody's voice and the sour expression that he held in his eyes.

"Ma'am, I've been through several, but none compare to the one."

An increasing tropical storm force wind was now crashing against the house, while lightning seared the Galveston sky. Water, in the form of a torrential driving rain and storm surge, was ravaging its way across the city. Marie's attention quickly shifted from staring at the ceiling and walls to denote the increasing severe weather to focusing back to Woody.

"The one? What do you mean 'the one'?"

"I mean the one that became a legacy for this island. Are you not aware of what happened here forty-three years ago this September?"

"No, I'm not," replied Marie, half-apologetic. "What happened?"

Amid flashes of lightning and the flickering of the oil lamp, Marie saw Woody's face fall from a stoic expression to a more sullen look. His face matched the expression he wore while caressing Amelia Franco's grave the day before, though

Marie didn't know this. Cautiously, sensing Woody's shift in mood, Marie asked again, "What happened?"

Caught off guard by how quickly forces were welling up within him, a couple of tears fell down his rugged sun creased cheeks. Astutely, he leaned forward towards Marie.

"Terror! On September 8, 1900, terror like no other struck this island. Every storm since reminds me of that horrific night and those painfully miserable days that followed."

As Woody spoke, quick flashbacks pierced through his mind—memories of water, wind, screams, debris, bodies, decay, smells, twisted carcasses, and broken lives. Woody flinched at the ghostly memories that vividly flashed in his mind.

"My Lord, that was such a dreadful night," Woody cracked. "To understand the scope of that night and the magnitude of what happened, let me set the stage for you. My name is Woodrow James Harris. I was an orphan and, upon growing up, I worked for the Sisters of Charity at St. Mary's Orphanage in maintaining the place. I was there when it all happened."

Chapter Three

Galveston in 1900 was a place of dreams. It was where the rich played and relaxed, and where many chose to make a life. A glorious city bolstered by the cotton industry, it boasted of a magnificent seaport that rivaled New York Harbor, and was a major port for immigration. Ships regularly arrived from Ireland, Poland, Germany, England, and France with immigrants all wanting to live the American dreams of freedom and prosperity. Galveston was believed to be a safe place to start a new life. Some even held the misguided belief that Galveston was a haven where the fiercest storm could never strike or harm anyone because its placement on the Texas Gulf Coast kept it protected; large storms would slide by to either the east or west, but never hit Galveston. In essence, Galveston, in the day, was like a royal queen, the star of the sea, an opulent jewel for all social classes.

Queen of the Waves

As always, the fourth of July was an extraordinarily festive time on the island. Murdock's Bathhouse was the usual center stage for most of the island's festivities. Couples and families flocked in and out of the palatial bathhouses and enjoyed the beach access, and refreshments. Celebrations for this Independence Day were even more fantastic because it was 1900. Galveston was in its prime in the start of a new century.

Further down the beach, to the west of Murdock's Bathhouse, St. Mary's Orphanage stood tall and proud, an imposing backdrop on the Texas Coastal plain. A group of ninety-three children laughed and played on the beach, enjoying their day in the sun. The children of St. Mary's Orphanage relished the afternoon's playtime; it was not often that they had days as carefree as this one.

"Mr. Clayton, look at the seashell I just found!" exclaimed Ruby Mae, as she came running from the beach's waterline.

"My, Ruby, that is a beautiful shell. It is a sand dollar. That's a very special shell. You hold onto that with extra care," beamed Nicholas Clayton.

"Ruby Mae, do you know what is so special about seashells?"

"No, Mr. Clayton. Is it because they are pretty?"

"Yes, sea shells are very pretty. But, they are special because they are a reminder to each of us that every life has something beautiful to offer this world."

Ruby was six years old and very precocious. She wanted to know as much as she could about everything. While Ruby was busy sharing her shells with Mr. Clayton, Susie and Agatha were crafting sand pies with their small fingers. A few feet away, Michael and John were building a sandcastle with their shovels. The boys' devotion to detail was noticed by Mr. Clayton, who sat down alongside the boys on the beach to offer his assistance. "You see, boys, you should consider better fortifying these outer walls like this."

Mr. Clayton scooped up wet sand and adhered it to the already existing walls of the boys' creation.

"This way, when the tide returns, your castle will still stand."

"Thanks, Mr. Clayton," said Michael.

The boys were thrilled with Mr. Clayton's feedback and they diligently shored up their exterior walls just as they were shown.

"We'll have to keep an eye on it and see if the tide takes it away."

Queen of the Waves

"Children, come and sit down for some ice cream," called Sister Mary Catherine. Almost as successful as trying to shepherd a flock of sea gulls, the Sisters managed to finally get the children seated together for a late afternoon snack.

"Father Kirwin, may I please have two scoops of ice cream?"

"Billy, how about if we start out with one scoop and after everyone's had a serving, we'll get you a second scoop."

"Okay, thank you, Father Kirwin."

"Woody, would you see about going to fetch another table and some more chairs so that the Claytons and others may also have a seat?"

"Yes, Father, right away."

"Father, that's quite thoughtful of you, but we are all quite alright. Please, let Woodrow enjoy this leisurely time as well."

"Mr. Clayton, you're a kind man to wish me comfort. I'm more than happy to go and fetch what is needed. I'll return shortly—I insist."

Mr. Clayton smiled warmly at Woody. "You're a good young man and I admire all you do for these children, for the Sisters, and for Father Kirwin here at St. Mary's."

Woody smiled shyly back at Mr. Clayton. Woody was the type who loved doing good deeds, but preferred to go about them as anonymously as possible. He definitely didn't like people making a big fuss over him, unless, it was Amelia Franco making the big fuss. Woody did, however, strongly appreciate and accept the warm compliment because it was given to him by Mr. Clayton—a man so accomplished and successful that Woody could not help but idolize him. After all, Nicholas J. Clayton was the essential architect of Galveston. Many of the churches, buildings, and homes in the city held his signature. Mr. Clayton was indeed a premiere architect not only in Galveston, but throughout Texas and many southern states. Despite a scrape with Galveston's city board over the design of the new courthouse, his architecture firm was doing well. But, the designs of the island's Victorian sandcastles weren't his only concern. Mr. Clayton loved his wife Lorena and their children, but he also concerned himself with the designs of the children at St. Mary's Orphan Asylum.

These children were the ultimate of hard luck cases. Most of the children found themselves tragically orphaned as a result of the Yellow Fever Epidemic that had spread uncontrollably throughout the island a few years ago. Losing both parents and having no family at such a tender age leaves a

Queen of the Waves

child with a deep void for their entire life. Nicholas Clayton identified with these children, including Woody, and the feelings they felt. He lost his father when he was only a little boy in Ireland. He understood the difficulties of growing up without a father. But, to also grow up without a mother's love was an entirely deeper tragedy. Thus, he loved to dote on these children and financed the orphanage in various ways. On this day, he made sure the children were going to celebrate July Fourth just like those at Murdock's. He made sure they had all the best foods to eat for a summer picnic—complete with ice cream, a novelty the children had only enjoyed once before. The spectacular surprise would be the fireworks Mr. Clayton procured for the children to enjoy just after sunset.

  The sea looked like a black iridescent pearl amid the moonlight. Red, blue, and silver chrysanthemums blossomed repeatedly in the night sky. The children ooooed and aaaahhhed at the flashes of light that shot out over the Gulf. Mr. Clayton beamed excitedly as he intently watched the children's reactions. Woody watched, too, with excitement at the fireworks display in between glances over at Amelia, his love, whom he would be marrying in just two short months. He didn't quite know how he was going to make enough money to provide for the both of them, but he believed love would show them the way.

"Woodrow, I've been thinking," spoke Nicholas in a relaxed fashion. "I'm in need of an extra person, an assistant, to help survey and photograph my construction sites. I was thinking you would make a fine assistant, given the reliable work you do for St. Mary's. It would help give you a bit more financial stability now that you are getting married."

Woody was shell-shocked by the incredible offer.

"Mr. Clayton, I've respected you for so long. I would be quite honored to be your assistant. However, I don't want to quit what I'm doing now."

"Woodrow, I was hoping you would accept. I will work with you to get a schedule adjusted and you could do both."

"Mr. Clayton, I'm quite obliged. How can I say no to a good deal like that? I accept."

"Woodrow, I'm pleased. Please come by my office next Monday and we can work out a schedule."

Woody could barely believe the opportunity that had just landed in his lap. He was given the golden ticket of opportunities—the chance to work with Nicholas Joseph Clayton, Texas' renowned architect. Woody struggled to contain the thrill he felt in his heart. Though normally composed, he allowed a small smile to spread across his face. He could now rest a little more assured that he would be able to provide more financial stability for Amelia and the family they hoped to have one day.

Just as Woodrow Harris found great pride in the work he did for St. Mary's Orphanage, Amelia Franco credited the orphanage with the good graces in her life. This special place is where she gained parents and discovered the love of her life. Though she knew Woodrow when they were children, it was only upon her return years later that she found her heart open to him. Amelia and Woody both felt that the beach and the buildings that comprised St. Mary's Orphanage were a sacred place and hallowed ground not only because of the nurturing holy work the ten Sisters of Charity provided the little ones, but because it simply was a place where love abounded. While the Sisters were strict in their teaching and childrearing, they deeply cherished all who entered. It was that love that kept the children happy and provided them with hope amid an otherwise lonely world. And, it was the radiance of the Sisters' deep spiritual love that infected others and inspired many to seek out lives of humble service in Galveston's community.

In the moonlight's pristine hue, Amelia looked prettier than a cherub, and Woodrow Harris could not take his eyes off of her. Amelia's white fitted dress cast a goddess like form to her silhouette as she stood facing the Gulf's sea breeze, gazing at the fireworks. Each color reflected brilliantly against her dress, which added further radiance to Amelia's complexion. At times, she wore a stoic expression and her elegant manner made her seem as statuesque as a patroness carved on the bow of a ship, guiding her sailors safely to port. Woody longed to go over to her and untie the navy ribbons on her matching white hat and remove the mother of pearl combs that were keeping her hair pinned in place. He longed to run his fingers through her lengthy black hair and just hold her. For a moment, he imagined everyone off the beach so that it was just the two of them in their own special moment in time. Beneath the grand celestial chandelier that was made of the moon and all the stars and planets, he indulged in the illusion of the beach being a private ballroom for their solitary use. He intently watched how her delicate pink lips stretched across her face in wave like form with every smile. The more he studied Amelia, the more he anticipated their nuptials. Catching him glancing at her, Amelia smiled largely at Woody and walked over to him, placing her hand in his hand.

"Isn't it splendid?" grinned Amelia, watching a firework and then glancing up into Woody's unwavering eyes.

"It sure is," he warmly replied, as he tenderly raised her hand and kissed it.

"I don't think I have ever seen anything more spectacular."

Realizing that Woody was not referring to the fireworks display, Amelia softly smiled and affectionately caressed his face. "Two more months until forever," she whispered.

"Yes, indeed, I cannot wait for you to be my bride."

Foolishly thinking they could steal a complete romantic moment with all the festivities going on around them, the illusion was broken.

"My dear Amelia, how are the wedding plans coming along?" asked Sister Elizabeth.

Amelia ignited brighter than one of the fireworks. "Plans are coming along quite well. Woody and I are set to marry on September eighth at three o'clock in the afternoon in St. Mary's Cathedral. My Aunt Mildred is sewing my dress. Mother and my other aunts will be so busy with all of the cooking for the luncheon afterward. Father Kirwin will be officiating our Matrimonial Mass.

"That all sounds quite lovely, Amelia. The two of you make a fine pair."

"Thank you, Sister."

"It's quite generous of you and Woodrow to include the children in your festivities."

"Woody and I wouldn't have it any other way. Those children are as much a part of our lives as if they are our own. We met because of them."

"The Holy Spirit is indeed guiding the both of you."

"Thank you, Sister. I pray it is so."

The inspired sandcastle Michael and John made with Mr. Clayton's help lasted for a week and two days. No one could have known how symbolic the sea's encroachment over the silicate creation would prove to be. In just eight weeks, Galveston and her inhabitants would fare a more perilous intrusion.

The time between July and September passed in hurried measure. The port was busy with ships coming in and out with various cargo, and to carry cotton to points all over the world. Galveston's port was an intricate helix of buyers, banks, shippers, factories, and merchants all feeding predominantly off of the cotton industry. As usual for this time of year, sailors arrived in port with harrowing stories about some grand storm they wrestled while at sea. Many of the pubs were filled in the late afternoons and evenings with all kinds of bawdy language as the sailors detailed how tall the waves were, how hard the

Queen of the Waves

wind blew, and how the crew almost perished. While many of the tales had some element of truth, it was nothing for a drunken sailor to add some extra details to make the story more interesting for the listener or even to outdo a story told by another sailor.

On the fourth day of September, shippers were wildly talking about a storm with incredible ferocity at the mouth of the Gulf of Mexico. Woody, who happened to be passing down the Strand on his way to take survey pictures for Nicholas Clayton's next site, heard some of the commotion. Feeling rather thirsty from the stifling day, Woody decided to drop in and listen to the latest talk. The bartender looked across the bar.

"Woodrow, what can I get for you?"

"I'll just have a sarsaparilla."

Woody wasn't one who liked to drink alcohol frequently. He occasionally dropped in and ordered a drink just so he could sit at the bar and listen to the various tales being spun. Listening to these tales was a form of mid-afternoon entertainment for him.

"The waves, I kid you not, were three times the height as the boat's masts. The ocean was swirling so and rocking about—that at times it seemed as if we was goin' to be upside down. All of my men were so sick. That wind just shredded the sails so that it looked like a bunch of ghouls were just flapping about above the ship. Truly this was a wicked mess of a gale."

Woody leaned in so he could hear more about what the Irish sounding sailor was saying. He was especially intrigued because it seemed everyone in shipping had been talking about a storm out at sea.

Taking a sip, Woody asked, "Excuse me, Sir, you talking about a storm?"

The boastful sailor, swaying a bit either due to alcohol, the effects of being at sea for a great period of time, or both, turned around to see who was asking him a question.

Seeing a hint of confused expression on the sailor's face, Woody repeated his inquiry. "Sir, did you mention you encountered a storm?"

"Why, yes, sir, I did. It was a hell of a storm, if I might say so. A monster. A possessed sea demon. A true beast!"

"My, where were you when you encountered this storm?"

"I and my crew were sailing back from England finishing a cotton run where we encountered this sea devil right at the mouth of the Gulf of Mexico. At first, we thought it would just be a usual summertime squall like

Queen of the Waves

what normally blows down there this time of year. But no, this—this was something more angry, more venomous than anything I've ever witnessed. Aye! The seas would rise up and curl like the mouth of an angry serpent and swallow vessels whole and leave them crushed."

"My goodness! What a frightful experience that had to be! Any news where the storm is going?"

"Some captains have been saying she'll blow over Cuba and into Florida. But, the truth is that a possessed demon like that will go anywhere it wants to thrash around and wreak havoc. Storms like that take on a life all their own."

"Well, as long as it doesn't come here. I'm getting married in just a few days. I sure don't want it raining on my pretty bride."

"Awwwwww, mate, that's wonderful." The jolly, animated sailor turned around to face the bar and its patrons, let out a shrill whistle, and hollered.

"Aye lads, this mate of ours is getting married in just four days. Let us raise him a cup of cheer!"

And with that, the men hollered and raised their glasses to Woody.

Woody bashfully nodded and smiled at the well wishers. The sailor slapped Woody on the back and wished him well with a hearty chuckle.

"No sir, you do not need to be worrying about any storm. You just focus on that bride of yours. You know how it is here in Galveston: we may get a gusty one now and again this time of year, but that's all. This port is a haven by the way it is protected—no real harm can ever come here."

With the sailor's buoyant words, Woody collected his gear and headed on to take survey pictures for Mr. Clayton. At the site survey, he shared the tales he heard about the storm, but most of the men dismissed it as folklore. Woody couldn't dismiss it. He had a feeling in his stomach that he could not shake—the feeling that something bad was about to happen. He had this feeling for a few days now, but he told himself it was just his nervousness about getting married. Upon reconsideration, deep down Woody knew he wasn't nervous at all about marrying his sweet Amelia. Marrying her was what he wanted more than anything. And yet, Woody was full of consternation—there was a dark feeling taking shadow over his joy.

September was a daunting month for the children because it meant the cessation of summer fun and time to begin

Queen of the Waves

a new course of studies. The Sisters were very strict and insistent upon academic excellence and structure at St. Mary's Orphanage. While the Sisters did their utmost in loving the children and providing them with the Lord's mercies amid the sad realities these children faced in not having parents or a family to support them, they also went to incredible lengths in raising these children's horizons by encouraging and expecting academic excellence. The hope was that each child could one day lead an extraordinary life and rise above society's stereotypes and mediocre expectations for those raised in orphanages.

The school days were a few hours a day; to the children, it sometimes felt like an eternity. They spent their hours learning religion, spelling, arithmetic, geography, handwriting, and reading. The girls and boys both enjoyed when the Sisters would take them on nature walks to explore the living creatures on the beach and in the water.

The girls were grouped together in one classroom while the boys were grouped together in another room. The girls usually were quite well-mannered, but the boys could be quite unruly at times. However, most of the antics happened between the boys and girls once they were in their dormitories.

Queen of the Waves

Sister Genevieve sternly stood tall and imposing before the boys.

"Boys, please take out your readers. Michael, please read Sir Walter Raleigh's poem, *The Passionate Man's Pilgrimage* on page nine."

"Yes, Sister.

The Passionate Man's Pilgrimage
Give me my scallop-shell of quiet
My staff of faith to walk upon,
My scrip of joy, immortal diet,
My bottle of salvation,
My gown of glory, hope's true gage;
And thus I'll take my pilgrimage.
Blood must be my body's balmer,
No other balm will there be given;
Whilst my soul, like a quiet palmer,
Travelleth towards the land of heaven;
Over the silver mountains,
Where spring the nectar fountains:
There will I kiss
The bowl of bliss;
And drink mine everlasting fill
Upon every milken hill:
My soul will be a-dry before;
But after, it will thirst no more
Then by that happy blestful day,
More peaceful pilgrims I shall see,
That have cast off their rags of clay,
And walk appareled fresh like me.

Queen of the Waves

I'll take them first
To quench their thirst,
And taste if nectar suckets,
At those clear wells
Where sweetness dwells
Drawn up by saints in crystal buckets.
And when our bottles and all we
Are filled with immortality,
Then the blessed paths we'll travel,
Strowed with rubies thick as gravel;
Ceilings of diamonds, sapphire floors,
High walls or coral, and pearly bowers.
From thence to heavens's bribeless hall,
Where no corrupted voices brawl;
No conscience molten into gold,
No forged accuser bought or sold,
No cause deferred, nor vain-spent journey;
For there Christ is the King's Attorney,
Who pleads for all without degrees,
And he hath angels, but no fees.
And when the grand twelve-million jury
Of our sins, with direful fury,
'Gainst our souls black verdicts give,
Christ pleads his death, and then we live.
Be thou speaker, taintless pleader,
Unblotted lawyer, true proceeder!
Thou giv'st salvation even for alms;
Not with a bribed lawyer's palms.
And this is my eternal plea
To him that made heaven, earth, and sea,
That, since my flesh must die so soon,
And want a head to dine next noon,
Just as the stroke, when my veins start and spread,

Queen of the Waves

Set on my soul an everlasting head.
Then am I ready, like a palmer fit;
To tread those blest paths which before I writ."

"Very good, Michael."

Michael smiled pleasantly upon hearing Sister Genevieve's satisfaction. A good student for fourteen years of age, Michael often found himself hearing more disdain from the Sisters than praise. If there was mischief to be made, Michael usually was at the center of it. He loved nothing more than the chance to torment the girls with pranks and antics, especially if it involved dried locust shells or a harmless grass snake.

"Class, this poem was written by Sir Walter Raleigh in 1604. What can you tell me about this poem that Michael just read? Nick, since you raised your hand first, you may speak."

"Well, Sister, this poem seems to be about death and the gentleman in the poem is making his peace with the thought that he is going to die."

"Very good, Nick. You are correct. Class, we must understand that death is a natural part of life. While we all hope that the good Lord gives us many years to enjoy this life we've been given, the truth is that the Lord uses us as an instrument to bring His love, hope, and mercy to others. However, at any

Queen of the Waves

time we can be called home to our Father in Heaven. Therefore, we must always strive to lead good and direct lives, as we never know when we may be going home to our divine Father. Class, since you all have been so diligent in getting your work done timely, let us recess for awhile onto the beach where we can enjoy this beautiful day the Lord has given us."

A twinkle gleamed in Michael's eye, as he instantly hatched a new plan, a new way to make Ruby Mae scream and all the girls along with her.

"Billy, Nick, Fred, come here! I have an idea. I was thinking that while the girls are in etiquette class, we could sneak some crabs into the dormitory. You know, hide them in their bed and then wait until later this evening to hear the scream."

"Yeah! That sounds too good," they all chimed.

Discreetly, Michael, Billy, Fred, and Nick collected hermit crabs on the beach and kept them hidden in a lunch pale they had lifted from the kitchen.

"Hey, Billy. What do you suppose crabs eat?" asked Fred.

"Hopefully, girls," said eight-year old Nick.

"Don't you think Sister Elizabeth is going to catch us?" squeaked Billy, always the second-guesser of the group.

Queen of the Waves

"No," said Michael, "It's perfect. I heard Sister Vincent say that she was going to be meeting with Sister Elizabeth for some discussion over tea. We have plenty of time to be in and out and then to make it to dinner without ever being detected."

"But what if Father Kirwin is dining with us tonight? He'd skin us alive. I'm not sure this is a good idea."

"Billy, don't be ridiculous; it'll be fine. Think how many times we've done these sort of runs before."

"Exactly, and look how many times we've been caught and gotten into trouble—every time!"

"Relax, won't you. It will be fine. Besides, it gives the Sisters something to talk about when we have all gone to sleep. You know they must be dying to have something to talk about after we've all gone to sleep. They are so reverent and all. You know that love they have for us shines through their anger and, after we've been punished, they sit around and probably laugh at some of the things we've done. After all, they are human too, remember?"

"Are they?" asked Billy.

"Of course they are," said Michael, as he playfully pushed Billy's shoulder.

With forty crabs collected, Michael, Billy, Fred, and Nick hid behind a cluster of pink oleanders and salt cedar trees

Queen of the Waves

waiting for the girls to go to etiquette class. They knew they were risking getting caught by being late to dinner, but they thought the calculated risk was worth it. Slowly, the boys tiptoed up the beautifully carpeted stairway of the girls' dormitory. The boys evenly distributed the defenseless hermit crabs between the beds, shoes, and closets. Quickly, they sneaked back down the stairs and ran out the back door while trying hard to not make a single sound."

"Hurry, let's get to dinner!" said Michael.

The boys quickly ran to the boys' dormitory. Before entering, they stopped to collect themselves and ensure that their shirts were tucked in and their hair was combed. They didn't want any evidence of mayhem. Guardedly, the boys crept to their places at the long dining room table, only to hear the voice of Sister Evangelist.

"Boys, where have you been?" quizzed Sister Evangelist.

"We...we...we...we were finishing our nature study," stammered Michael.

"All right then. Be sure to eat your vegetables. No hiding them under your plates."

Billy looked across the table at Michael, at Nick, and then Fred in disbelief that they actually had gotten away with

69

being late to dinner. Before long, the children found themselves getting ready for bed. All at once, a multitude of loud screams bellowed from the girls' dormitory. Indeed, the relocated crabs had been found. The boys involved could not help but laugh, laughing until their faces were a purplish shade of red. They tried to contain their amusement by burying their faces into their pillows, but it was of no use. It wasn't long before Sister Camillus and Sister Elizabeth charged into the room and yanked each of the four boys out of bed.

"What on Earth were you boys thinking? March across there now and clean up the mess you made. You will then be responsible for scrubbing the floors in the morning. Tell the girls you are sorry."

"But, how do you know it was us," stammered Michael in an almost whiny voice.

"Because Sister Evangelist marked you all as tardy to dinner. You boys thought you had gotten away with it; didn't you?"

"Yes, Sister Camillus," the boys said in a defeated tone in unison while looking at the wooden floor.

"Now, march over there and apologize to the girls."

The boys went over to the girl's dormitory and collected the wayward crabs and, half smirking, apologized to the girls. But, the truth is that they were not sorry in the least. The boys reveled in the moment of causing the girls such irritation.

The Sisters worked hard to keep order for the children, and yet moments like this would bring them secret amusement. Certainly, with such a range in ages, the orphanage was never a dull place. The Sisters always had their hands full and they gave thanks to the Lord for every moment they had with these precious children.

Queen of the Waves

Chapter Four

The wind was an invisible razor slicing through anything that came up against it. A loud rolling crash shook Marie and Woody. It sounded as though the roof was falling in above them. The trees violently flailed back and forth in a circular motion. Roofing tiles and loose debris hurled through the stormy air.

"What on Earth was that?" asked Marie in a most apprehensive voice. The wind speed continued to rise, causing a high-pitched wailing noise. Marie grabbed the lantern. Lightening pierced through the torrential rain. The wind blew hard against Marie's house, lashing the trees. Marie grew even more frightened by the sheer force of the wind. The walls, roof, and ceiling all popped and moaned as they were shaken by the wind. At times, a gust would seem so strong that Marie feared, at any moment, she would surely lose her roof. A muffled engine-like sound was heard in between the roaring thunder and overwhelming wind.

"It's really blowing out there," said Woody in an almost monotone voice.

"Yes, it is," Marie said in an extremely nervous tone.

"Woodrow, is that a plane I hear or the sound of the wind?"

"Ma'am, I'm not quite sure. I can't imagine a plane in the air right now."

"Gosh, now would be a horrible time for the Germans to attack us. You know they've been saying that a German submarine was reported just off the bay the other day. Oh, how dreadful if we are about to be attacked or invaded. I'm not sure I'd know whatever to do if this is the case. How I wish my dear Charlie was here. He'd know exactly what to do. His pistol is in the cupboard drawer. Perhaps I should get it."

"Ma'am. Marie. I do believe I hear a plane like you said. How could a plane be flying in this raging storm? A plane flying in this—it don't make sense. Maybe we are about to be attacked. I'm surprised the sirens aren't going off. Guess they don't have to worry about sanctioning a blackout because the storm has taken care of that for them."

"Here is Charlie's pistol and riffle," said Marie, walking back into the faint candle lit living room with a gun in each hand."

"That's great, Marie; but these guns won't take out what that plane may be dropping."

"No, it won't. But, it will have to do for whatever monster comes out of the sea and to my door."

Wearing a serious expression, Marie placed the pistol on the gray, pink, and black swirled marble top of the end table beside the sofa and laid the riffle across the mantle of the fireplace. In the event these weapons would be needed to defend an attack, they were in an easy place to grab and go. She looked around the room. Noticing the increasing dimness, she lit a few more candles to add more light to the darkness. Nature was moving—a force set into motion. There was no stopping it and, while she tried desperately to put on a brave face, it was the feeling of powerlessness that frightened Marie to her core.

"Now, Woody, why don't you tell me more about the Galveston that was and this storm you were talking about or leading to?"

"Yes, Ma'am. I'd be obliged to fill in the rest of the story."

"I believe you left off with you and Amelia getting close to your wedding. date."

Chapter Five

At long last, it was the weekend Amelia and Woody had been looking forward to, the weekend they were to be married in St. Mary's Cathedral. It was the morning of September 8, and Woody could not imagine himself ever happier than the joy he was feeling inside that morning. He was hours away from marrying his sweet Amelia, the sweet angel the Lord sent into his life. Father Kirwin had celebrated morning Mass in the orphanage's chapel for the Feast of Our Lady's Nativity. The rest of Woody's morning was to be spent running into town to fetch some rope, nails, and wood to mend the fences along the orphanage property before finishing final wedding details. He was counting down the minutes until Amelia would become his beloved bride.

"Woodrow, while you are in town getting supplies, please stop at the infirmary and call back Sister Elizabeth. I'm concerned about the rising sea and I think we may need her

Queen of the Waves

help with the children this afternoon. It is looking like we may be in for some kind of squall today. Hopefully, this will all pass and reveal a blessed afternoon for your wedding."

"Yes, Sister. I sure hope so."

As Woody was hitching the horse, Tess, to the buggy, he noticed the unusual surf continuing to build. The waves were quite tall and crashing to the shore like one would see from a strong tempest. But, it was the most consternating of circumstances that boggled his mind because the sky was not threatening. The sky was ashen gray and, though it was cloudy, there was hardly an angry cloud in the heavens. He watched the ocean for a little while and found that it actually startled him a bit. He trusted that all would be fine because the sky didn't have a threatening appearance to it, but decided he would talk to Mr. Cline, the resident meteorologist, about the unusual tides when he got into town. It wasn't long before the children also began to notice the unusually large crashing waves.

"Woody, you going into town?"

"Yes, Michael, Sister Camillus is sending me to get Sister Elizabeth. I'm also going to go fetch some supplies to mend those fences so they'll be in good shape before tomorrow. I want things in good shape before I leave with Amelia tomorrow for our honeymoon in New Orleans."

Queen of the Waves

"Woody, do you see those waves? Sister Vincent and Sister Mary were talking about them and wondering about the unusual tide. I think it's making Sister Vincent uneasy. I heard her humming *Queen of the Waves* under her breath. So can I go with you into town to get Sister Elizabeth?"

"Did you get permission from one of the Sisters?"

"Sister Vincent, can I go with Woody into town to help get Sister Elizabeth?"

"Yes, Michael, that would be rather nice for you to help Woodrow," said Sister Vincent Cottier, who had come out on the front veranda of the boys' dormitory to catch another glimpse of the rough surf.

The three mile ride into town turned out to be quite a journey. The surf was rough and slowly rising, causing minor flooding on some of the main roads. Almost out of nowhere, the sky became overrun with heavy coal black clouds that seemed so bottom heavy over the Gulf waters that they looked as though they were scraping against the troubled surf. It began to lightly rain. At times, Woody had to yell at Tess because she was spooked by the shallow tidal waters coming in over the sandy dirt road and did not want to budge any further. Woody began to doubt his earlier assumption that the weather would be fine.

Queen of the Waves

It was a half past nine in the morning when Woody and Michael reached the Tremont Hotel in the heart of Galveston's commerce district. Water was covering all the streets close to the port and the water appeared to be rising.

While securing the horse to a post, Woody saw Mr. Smith, one of Mr. Clayton's contractors, walking out of the hotel with a group of business men, and hollered to him.

"Hello, Mr. Smith."

"Hello, Mr. Harris."

"Do you know what is going on with the tides? Why this flooding is happening? Is there a storm coming?"

Right upon the utterance of the last question, Woody abruptly remembered the bawdy sailors in the pub days earlier talking about a monster storm and how it was like a demon trying to possess their ships out at sea. A sick feeling eclipsed Woody's heart; it shot down his spine, pierced his gut, and lacerated his soul. His blood instantaneously ran cold. All color fell from his face.

"Woodrow, I'm hearing that all should be okay. Nothing to worry about at all."

"Thank you, Mr. Smith."

The bad feeling Woody had put aside had returned and was now pressing on his heart, making it difficult for him to breath. Despite what Mr. Smith said, Woody knew that something dark was on the eve of happening. While he could not stop what he feared was about to happen, he could at least warn those that he loved. Seeing men in their rolled up trousers and women with raised skirts and petticoats frolicking in the flood waters and even swimming in the flooding roadways, Woody grabbed hold of Michael, who was just about to dive into the mucky tidal surge.

"Woody, I just want to swim like the others!"

"No, Michael. We have some business to take care of and then we have to get back to the Sisters!"

Woody quickly ran into the trade store and bought some rope, twine, six pieces of lumber, some nails, three lanterns, and lantern oil. He also fetched some fresh fruit from the market. It was now a little after eleven in the morning and three feet of water was covering every portion of Galveston. He and Michael stopped at St. Mary's Infirmary, but were told that Sister Elizabeth had left moments earlier for the orphanage on horseback. A steady rain was falling with periodic strong gusts of wind. Woody turned the buggy around and raced westward for the orphanage as quickly and skillfully as he could through the rising water. Along the way, he stopped by the Franco home to warn his Amelia and her family of his concern that a serious storm was coming. Mr. Franco, instead of heading the warning and concern, insisted that the extremely high tides would be a passing phenomenon and all would be well by three o'clock. Disappointed by Mr. Franco's dismissal of the warnings, Woody cut the visit short to ensure he and Michael would still be able to return to the orphanage through the ever-rising surf. They found the water steadily getting higher the nearer they were to the orphanage. The water was moving water—water that was becoming increasingly forceful and beginning to topple small trees and minor structures. By the time Woody approached the orphanage, he could not believe what he saw.

"Woody, look at that, the water is almost all the way around our buildings. See how the waves are hitting the cypress trees? I've never seen that happen before."

"Yes, Michael, I see that. We're going to have to stop here and negotiate our way carefully through the water."

"What about Tess?"

"We're going to have to leave her here and free her to be able to run or swim. I can't make her go any further. Our cart already is starting to take on water. It will soon float away. We have no choice, but to let it and Tess go."

With Tess bucking to get free and to get to higher ground, Woody was unable to grab much except the ball of rope and a lantern before the horse bolted while still attached to the cart. Carefully, Woody and Michael waded through the four to five feet of moving water and even swam a bit at times. Fortunately, they were able to get to the steps of the orphanage without being swept out into the ocean or having a wave knock them into a structure or below the surface of the water. Sister Raphael came running out with towels and grabbed hold of Michael and rushed him inside. Sister Evangelist and Sister Catherine both helped Woody up the steps of the boys' dormitory.

"Here, give me the lantern and that ball of rope," said Sister Catherine. "How blessed you are that you weren't swept out to sea!"

It was not long after Woodrow's return that Sister Camillus was plucking Sister Elizabeth out of the swiftly rising water. Sister Elizabeth was soaked and her nerves were quite shaken.

"I didn't think I'd make it back in time! The water in town is rising so dramatically, as it is all around here. Buildings along the seashore on the east are collapsing from the waves, as are bathhouses, piers, and hotels. Boats are

Queen of the Waves

loosening from their moorings and beginning to smash into other buildings or homes. All kinds of mayhem is happening in town. Houses are being inundated with feet of water. I saw a cow trying to take shelter on Mrs. Bingham's front porch," said Sister Elizabeth in an excited, but controlled tone.

Sister Camillus looked even more stunned and rattled. "Mrs. Bingham doesn't have cattle."

"I know. That's my point. It is getting desperate all around us. Sister Camillus, with these waves now crashing near our buildings, I am concerned for the welfare of the children and us. As we speak now, look how the water is rising up the steps. It won't be long and the water certainly will be pouring in here. Look how it already is lapping halfway up the steps to the porch. See, too, how the dunes are eroding. This place was fortunate to weather the storm of '75, but I have grave concern for what may be about to happen. We need to take immediate action and gather everyone together and move immediately to the chapel in the girls' dormitory. We will be safe there. The building is newer."

"Yes, Sister, I agree with you. I will gather the children, staff, and the other Sisters."

"Good. I will go and gather up as many supplies as I can. We must make haste. The talk in town before I evacuated was that Mr. Cline was seen riding his horse across the beachfronts warning people that a cyclone is coming. Sister, let us pray that the Lord's mercy will be with us as we dutifully guard these children this day."

While the Sisters, Woody, and staff carefully moved the children through the ever-surging tide to the girls' dormitory, Sister Elizabeth frantically ran through the cupboards and gathered together a basket of two-day old fruit, a loaf of bread, a jug of drinking water, a knife, and a neatly wound ball of clothesline. Bravely, Sister Elizabeth negotiated her way through the rising surf to join the others in the chapel of the girls' dormitory. Woody wished he could send further word to Amelia and prayed she and her family would not be in harm's way. Woody knew there would be no wedding today, and he grimly began to wonder if there even would be a tomorrow.

About three in the afternoon, the increasing wind velocity steadily began to drive torrents of rain against the Victorian city. The muddy silt laden waters foamed with rage. Large frothy waves slashed at the coastal plain. The foam collected on the waterline in mounds. Perpetually, the waves would return and disperse the sea foam only for it to recollect further inward beyond the beach—and so this process continued until the entire beach and city were completely submerged by over ten feet of water. Boats were loosened from their moorings and tossed onto Broadway, the city's main thoroughfare. The darkness of the sky matched the midnight opalesque waters. The storm began to ire so fiercely that one could not deny that evil was in the air. By five o'clock, the maniacal wheel of death hurled itself closer to shore. Buildings and other structures toppled by nature's fury and then turned into battering rams and slammed into other structures and people.

It was approximately half past five in the afternoon when, out of the darkness, the children and Sisters all heard several violently loud crashes and splashes outside amid the movement of the water. It was the sound of the boys' dormitory collapsing a hundred feet away from the girls' dormitory where they were housed. More loud noises emanated from outside of the girls' dormitory. The stripped wooden boards and slats that once constituted the boys' dormitory slammed perpetually against the girls' dormitory. All at once, water invaded and climbed up the burgundy carpeted stairs inside the girls' dormitory into the chapel, while the incensed sea serpent swiped out the chapel's jewel-toned stained glass image of the Annunciation. The children screamed and clung to the Sisters. In immediate reaction, the staff and Sisters Vincent,

Queen of the Waves

Elizabeth, Evangelist, Genevieve, Catherine, Raphael, Felicitas, Benignus, and Finbar grabbed the children and evacuated further up the stairs to the second floor. With the other Sisters grabbing the children to flee for safety, Sister Camillus rushed the ciborium of the Blessed Sacrament out of the tabernacle and carried it upstairs with the others for safe keeping. Each Sister worked hard within herself to keep a face that spoke of faith and not of fear.

"Children, let us remember that God in Heaven loves us. And as Jesus told Peter: Be not afraid. We, too, shall walk in this storm with the Lord. Come, children, let us pray the *Our Father*."

As evening fell upon Galveston, the children were petrified by all the destruction that was going on around them. Though the Sisters were soothing them and telling them not to be scared, they could not help but be scared. They had heard the collapsing of the boys' dormitory, the stables, and some other buildings around them. They had just witnessed the Gulf's waters pour into the chapel and the stained glass windows blow out before being evacuated to the second floor. They could hear the howling wind and feel the vibrations of the wicked waves smashing chunks of other buildings into the sides of the girls' dormitory. They could feel the ocean churning beneath them as the building began to sway. They knew they were all in impending danger. The Sisters too were terrified, but they found inside themselves the grace to be strong and brave. These little life forces had been entrusted to them and it was their duty as part of God's will to be good and valiant stewards to the end—however the end may present itself.

"Children, let us pray that the Lord will protect us, and that Our Lady will intercede on our behalf and send God's mercies down upon us."

It was a spiral of demons that screamed mercilessly upon their descent; their nails sharper than rapiers slashed recklessly through the bejeweled town. And so it began…the height of the storm was thrust upon Galveston. The venomous sea serpent like storm lashed out in full-primal fury, wielding powerful blows to the city. Palm trees, oak trees, pecan trees, cedar trees, magnolia trees all bent back and forth in an unyielding death grip before being snapped, twisted, and thrown lifelessly to the earth. Electric lines were ripped apart effortlessly. If it wasn't by the sheer force of the water, the serpent's warm steamy breath pummeled houses, threw a locomotive off of its tracks, crushed lives, snatched souls, and annihilated a city. There was little mercy to be found. As

Queen of the Waves

people fled from a derailed train into the lighthouse on Bolivar Peninsula to seek desperate refuge, the sea beast slammed water inside the lighthouse and swiped away several more souls.

The claws of death began to snatch away at the girls' dormitory at St. Mary's Orphanage. Having retreated finally to the attic, the children were all screaming in great despair and panic. All of the levels below them were filled with the Gulf's massive stormy surge.

"Children, be not afraid. Let us have faith. We are going to take the clothesline and tie it around you and then tie you to us so that, in the event that we end up in the water, you will be able to stay with us," said Sister Elizabeth, as she quickly cut up clothesline for the Sisters to use. Each Sister took nine children, fastened clothesline around their little waists to the cincture on the Sister's habit.

"Come children, let us sing together *Queen of the Waves*:

> Queen of the Waves, look forth across the ocean
> From north to south, from east to stormy west,
> See how the waters with tumultuous motion rise
> Up and foam without a pause or rest.
> But fear we not, tho' storm clouds round us gather,
> Thou art our Mother and thy little Child
> Is the All Merciful, our loving Brother

Queen of the Waves

God of the sea and of the tempest wild.
Help, then sweet Queen, in our exceeding danger,
By thy seven griefs, in pity Lady save;
Think of the Babe that slept within the manger
And help us now, dear Lady of the Wave.
Up to the shrine we look and see the glimmer
Thy votive lamp sheds down on us afar;
Light of our eyes, oh let it ne'er grow dimmer,
Till in the sky we hail the morning star.
Then joyful hearts shall kneel around thine altar.
And grateful psalms reecho down the nave;
Never our faith in thy sweet power can falter,
Mother of God, our Lady of the Wave."

In a blinding flash of lightning, and a sudden force of hysterical wind and towering waves, while the children and Sisters were singing, the walls of the girls' dormitory collapsed. The wind howled as it threw stinging darts of rain. In an instant, the beautiful place for children, this beacon of hope for the young, was gone, and so too were the Sisters and most of the children and staff. As the relentless motion of the waves drowned the children, the weight was too much for the Sisters to bear, as they fought the force of the surf and smashing debris with the children tied to them.

I managed to grab onto a door that was floating in the water and pulled myself up. I held on for my life. Still, I was flailing around in the water looking for any sign of life, but

Queen of the Waves

there was none that I could see. The pulsating lightning flashes were the only light I had in hopes of seeing someone. There was no way to tell where I was for a long while because of the way the storm was blowing and swirling around everything. People were dying savage deaths by either drowning or from being hit by debris flying through the air. The sounds around me were immense—the resounding thunder, shrill screeching of the wind, the relentless shhhhhhhing sound of the tempestuous water, the battering of houses and other structures collapsing and then catapulting into other houses and buildings, the agonizing half-muted screams of those enduring pain and crying out for help. These are sounds your mind never forgets. Though it happened so long ago, I still can hear it as if it just now happened. The entire course of the night, I spent not only trying to survive, but praying that my Amelia was safe. I worried about her and her family. I prayed that there would still be a day where I would be marrying my Beloved. I remember how in a series of flashes of lightning I could see that I was taken all the way out from the orphanage on the west side of the island and had been swept at least six miles to the east side beyond St. Mary's Cathedral. Amid the flashes, I could see the statue of Mary standing on the small dome of the cathedral, arms stretched out. It was then that I began to cry. The Holy

Queen of the Waves

Mother was my beacon in this hopeless situation, marking where I was in the same moment the gravity of all that was lost was weighing upon me. She truly was my angel of mercy. It was in seeing her that I found the strength to hold on a bit tighter and to continue to fight as hard as I could to stay alive while I became increasingly aware that the city I loved was no more—it had been destroyed, and many of the people I knew and cared for may have been lost forever.

By six in the morning, the storm began to let up and much of the wild surf was beginning to subside and settle. I was able to grab a board and, using it as an oar, negotiated my way further into town. I got to the beginning of Avenue O where the water had subsided to being waist deep. I waded as quickly as I could through the water, and climbed over towering piles of debris as best as I could to get to Amelia's house. The rain was still falling, but, thankfully, the largest battering waves had ceased. I was desperate to see her and know that she was okay—that she was still alive. Unfathomable destruction was everywhere. Bodies, bloating in the salt water, were floating in the water, and unrecognizable in most cases. A dead horse was wrapped around a mammoth pecan tree that was still somehow rooted in the ground. Where houses once prominently stood, there was now nothing but

Queen of the Waves

rubble. As more daylight began to filter through the clouded sky, I could see the skeleton of Amelia's home. The roof had been blown off the home completely. The prominent front porch where we often sat was stripped away from the house. Water was standing at least four feet inside the remains of the home. I waded into the house to find Amelia's parents floating face first in the water. A large oak tree had fallen onto Mr. Franco causing him to be pinned beneath the water. Mrs. Franco, too, had drowned. Holding back my worst fears, I frantically waded through the house looking for my Amelia and hollering her name. She was nowhere to be found. I waded into the back of her house and started digging through the muddy water and wreckage. There she was. A force I never felt before in my life came screeching out of my lungs. It was the loudest sound I ever heard; it was the sound of my crying out, "No!" My precious, beautiful Amelia had been pierced through the heart by a board. I cried out shrilly and hysterically. "No!" I dug deeper to further free her body. As I freed her, I could tell she had been gone for several hours. The day that was supposed to be our wedding day had gone so wrong. It instead was the day that she died. I pulled the piece of timber from her body carefully and just held her in my arms. Again, I was hysterically crying out "No!" I thought, 'How could God take this precious angel from me?' The enormity of the moment crashed upon me like a tsunami. This horrific storm not only swept away my home, my livelihood, but it robbed me of the love of my life, my purpose for living. I held Amelia and cried a howling horrific cry. I made sounds I didn't know I was capable of making; I was in that much pain. The home I built for Amelia and me to live in on Avenue N, close to 35th Street was destroyed as well. I had spent years saving up money to build Amelia a proper home and then several more months of our engagement building the home with my own hands. Mr. Clayton helped me with the design. Every now and then, some friends from church would help in constructing it, but mostly the work was done by my hands. It was all for Amelia, to show her how much I love her. Now, it was all gone, completely swept away. So suddenly, I was utterly alone.

Above all of the surrounding chaos, I heard a frantic shuffling through the water in the street. I looked and saw Mr. Clayton. Realizing that I could not do anything for Amelia or her family, I tenderly set Amelia down and hurried to see if Mr. Clayton needed help. He was rushing as quickly as he could through the water and mounds of debris to get to his wife Lorena and their precious children. Mr. Clayton had been caught off guard by the storm's surge while trying to meet a

Queen of the Waves

deadline and was forced to weather the deadly storm in his office.

Fortunately, Mr. Clayton faired better than most. His family survived the storm. But, Mr. Clayton suffered a different type of loss. Many of the beautiful buildings he designed were wiped away, while others were badly damaged in the stroke of one brush of wild nature, as though he had only designed sandcastles for the sea to devour. What many people don't understand is that for an architect to see his finished building means that all of his passion and efforts are present in a tangible state, much like a writer to a novel or a painter to a painting. It's expressed beauty that's meant to be shared. The moment that the object of beauty is destroyed, especially in large detail, deep pain immediately is inflicted upon the creator of such work. While Mr. Clayton was able to reunite with his doting wife and adoring children, and some of his structures survived, much of him was lost in the storm. Mr. Clayton had said that all of the destruction was like daggers to his soul. However, he was most distressed by the loss of the precious children and Sisters at the orphanage whom he loved to spoil. This storm triggered the final act of his architectural career and his health.

Queen of the Waves

My wedding day. What was supposed to be my wedding day was instead an infamous day, a day in which I felt like I was part of the walking dead. I began to think that maybe those corpses I saw lying in the rubble or floating in the water were the lucky ones. Though I was alive and breathing, I felt like I was dead. Everything had so suddenly been ripped away from me. Such overwhelming destruction, death, and loss surrounded me that I could not quite wrap my mind around it all. I was in a complete state of emotional paralysis. I had gone from living in a simple paradise to a complete hell in the fury of one night. It was complete carnage as far as the eye could see. I was just one soul in a cast of thousands suffering the agony of loss. I, too, might as well have been struck with a piece of timber because I felt as though I had been mortally impaled. I faced the daunting task of pulling myself together and living through the difficult days that were to come, without my Beloved.

Chapter Six

The thunder reverberated as loud as cannon fire, and the driving rain pelted the house. Marie sat on her sage green tapestry sofa across from Woody, staring at him in numbed silence. Tears cascaded down her face. Marie felt more than stunned. She felt overwhelming sadness and emotion for all that Woody had revealed to her. Her heart broke for this man who sat facing her. She could tell on the first day she met him that there was a story in those tired eyes, and now she had been proven correct in her judgment. The steely ice blue eyes contained a tragic story of love and immense loss. Marie wanted to embrace the man in consolation, but then thought it awkward. She wanted to do something for this poor soul, but all she could do was wipe the tears from her own eyes.

"I'm so sorry for your loss, for the horror that you had to endure," said Marie, with a voice that wavered with the gripping sorrow she was trying to settle inside of her.

"Everything was just torn from you in just mere hours. You lost absolutely everything."

"Yes," said Woody, wearing a somber, but stiff expression. "It's been many years since I've told my story to anyone. In fact, I don't remember the last time I've done such a thing. I usually keep it all to myself. I figure most people would not understand or care about the horror of that night or the agony in the days that followed."

Wearing an expression as if she'd seen a phantom, Marie's mind flashed to the names on the graves she had cleaned. All of a sudden, the curious pieces that Marie had puzzled over these last few weeks suddenly fit to form a tragic mosaic in her mind.

"All of them, all of these people were killed. Your Amelia, Ruby Mae, the Sisters, the children—they were all killed. They are the ones whose graves I have been cleaning, aren't they?"

With a somber, but warm expression in his eyes, Woody nodded his head slowly up and down. "Yes, those beautiful souls were the fabric of my life, and I've spent all of this remaining time praying for them and watching over them."

Marie's eyes welled up with even more tears, as she slowly raised her right hand to cover her mouth in the midst of the stunning realization. She now knew the full story surrounding all of those markers she found and what significant event had occurred on September 8, 1900.

A tremendous moan came from outside that was followed by an even louder crashing sound. The loud, abrupt noises caused Marie to whence in alarm by the sounds. Deeply moved by all Woody had shared with her, she wiped the fountain of tears pouring from her eyes. She felt overwhelmed by the gravity of the moment. An even greater noise came from the backyard. Regaining a surge of adrenaline, Marie bolted off the sofa to see what was happening. She hastened into the kitchen and opened a shutter in time to see the trees swishing and whipping around in the storm. A powerful rush of wind unexpectedly rose up and blew out the kitchen windows with one shattering force in the same instant Marie queried if the shutters could hold in the storm. "Aaaaaaahhhhh." Marie cried out in alarm. She scurried backward to crouch down by the stove and wall in order to shield herself from further flying glass and debris.

"Ma'am. You really shouldn't be in here with this storm raging as it is," said Woody, reaching to refasten the kitchen storm shutters. Tugging gently on Marie's arm, he led her out of the kitchen by lantern light. It was only a little after seven o'clock in the evening, but the darkness created the illusion that it was much later.

"Where are we the safest? I've never been through anything like this before."

Just then, the sounds of crashing glass could be heard upstairs. Panic surged through Marie, especially after hearing the story Woody just told her.

"Ma'am, let's stay here in your sitting room in this corner. We'll be right fine over here." The briskness of Woody's voice softened to comfort the fear he realized was going through Marie.

"Yes, Ma'am. This right here is pretty serious stuff. This ain't just a thunderstorm. Like I said, I've seen this before."

"Do you really think this is a hurricane?"

"Yes'm I do."

"Do you hear that? It sounds like an airplane again. That doesn't make sense. Why would a plane be flying in this? Something is not right. With all the sirens they've been testing and the blackout drills they've been planning in case the Germans come calling, looking to bring the war here—wouldn't we be told about an approaching hurricane? Surely that was just the wind roaring like a plane."

Queen of the Waves

"Marie, I don't know. I do know that the government is capable of many things. We are at war—so the possibilities are endless."

"There it goes again. I hope it's not a German plane we're hearing that's about to unleash a fury of bombs on us!"

The complete powerlessness of the situation encroached over Marie and devoured her nervous system. Never in her life had Marie been more scared than she was in this moment. She fought to remain calm. A storm raged out of control, an airplane seemed to be circling—perhaps to bring war on the shores of the U.S. Gulf Coast, and her Beloved was thousands of miles away and his safety was unknown. Trying to calm her nervously racing heart, Marie, almost breathless, surveyed the room in the flickering candle light. Her eyes traced from the far wall where her sofa was to the antique mahogany and marbled end tables and the blue and sage Tiffany-style lamps that sat on them. Her eyes then traced over to the opposite wall and cautiously perused the bricks of the fireplace. Her eyes fixed on the mantle and the eight inch by ten inch portrait of her Charlie. She could not take her eyes off his picture in the dim flickering light. She sat there, captivated by the image of him beaming back at her. The picture of Charlie evoked calmness over her like a lighthouse beacon to a storm weary sailor on a

Queen of the Waves

violent sea. More thrashing, banging, crashing, and knocking sounds were coming from all around the exterior of the house. In one quick movement, Marie dashed to the mantle, grabbed the picture of her husband, and then hurried back to her chair. She set the picture of Charlie on the round mahogany carved gaming table that was between Woody and her. With the lantern light flickering, she gazed at the picture. It brought an even greater sense of peace to her fear. Except for one solitary tear that coasted down Marie's right cheek, a smile emerged while she stared at the image of her Charlie in his Sunday suit.

"You miss him." Woody's gruff voice startled Marie, breaking her temporary spell of bliss.

"Yes, I miss him terribly, especially, right now. I wish he was here with me. I wish he was here and could wrap his arms around me and tell me that everything will be okay. He was always so good at holding me when I was afraid or upset about something. He would just hold me and I would just look up into those deep blue eyes and see that gentle sideways smile of his. Then, I would know that everything would be alright because he was there to watch over me. In the worst of troubles, those blue eyes were my blue skies. He always saw me through things and never broke a promise. He's the love of my...."

Marie's voice broke and she sobbed. She buried her face in her hands to shield herself from the deluge of emotions gripping her. She felt as though she was stuck in a vortex with layers of wickedness and many unknowns swirling about her. She had no idea what would be happening next on any level. But, she knew whatever the future held, she'd have to be strong and brave it on her own terms, as that's what Charlie would want her to do.

Understanding the heartbreak she was suffering, Woody reached his aged, wrinkled hand across the table and placed it on top of Marie's hand that was now griping the table as though she was holding on for her life's sake.

"I understand the tears and your sadness. I guarantee this will all pass. Tomorrow will be a new day, and the morning star will dawn with her perpetual hope. You will look around you, see what is broken, and, picking up the pieces, you will take a step closer to realizing your prayers. Don't let go of the hope that is inside of you. Live in the love you have. No one, not Hitler and his Nazi forces, a world at war, communism, the relentless oppressions and atrocities this world yields, or even the relentless force of a hurricane can take away the love inside of you. No one can strip away from you what is in your heart. Remember that love conquers all and

Queen of the Waves

is the reason to keep on living and fighting for your life. Remember my talking about Mr. Clayton? Despite all of his serious losses, he did as best he could to revel in the blessing that his family survived the mighty storm. As tight as money was for Mr. Clayton, he continued to contribute to St. Mary's Cathedral, St. Patrick's, and the re-established St. Mary's Orphanage, and doted on those children who came to live there until his health began to fail him. He didn't have much, but Mr. Clayton lived in love. While you have no control over your husband's safety or how this storm will play out, embrace yourself now in his living legacy, which is clearly his love for you. Live in love. As long as you live in love, it will make all of the coming tragedies, trials, and tribulations easier for you to endure. I believe your husband will be coming home to you because he's out there living in his love for you. With the two of you living in love for one another, hope remains. Be a witness of God's unfailing love to this war ravaged world. Be a beacon of light to those lost in the storm. Don't ever become so daunted that you cannot bear the light of the morning star."

  Mrs. Covington's tears stopped falling and she found herself wondering how this man, who spoke so brusquely days ago, had suddenly taken on the voice of an angel. His words touched her profoundly. In fact, Woodrow's words had such a deep impact on her that she no longer felt frightened; she felt empowered.

"Thank you, Woody, for your most inspired words. Can you tell me—how was it for you? The sun rose the next day—how did you pick up the pieces and move forward?"

Chapter Seven

The immediate days that followed September 8, 1900, were excruciating. If you weren't dead, then at times you wished you were. Thousands upon thousands of human corpses lay rotting and decaying in the saline air. Hundreds upon hundreds of people were injured. I could not comprehend what my eyes were telling me. Everywhere I looked there was ruin. The city's landscape was a mountainous range of debris that stretched for miles. Buildings and homes that I passed everyday had been reduced to battered lumber and mangled bits strewn in mounds several feet tall. Bodies, too, were thrown and laying about all over the island like lifeless rag dolls. Indeed, the weeks that followed were arduous, exhausting, and numbing.

The air hung heavy, which added to the misery of the stagnant and stifling heat. What were once major thoroughfares were now heavily blocked with electrical and telegraph poles, timbers, slate, glass, paper, sewage, and all kinds of other materials. There was barely a habitable house left in the city, as very few homes survived the mammoth storm. For the most part, all business structures had been severely damaged. The streets were full of anguished and famished survivors who wandered around dazedly dumbstruck by the momentous tragedy that had occurred. Schools had been ruined and countless churches and synagogues were leveled. The factories, warehouses, and grain elevators that were central to the city's economy were all destroyed. All bridges leading on and off the island were swept away. Ships were tossed across town onto roadways as if they were merely toys leftover from a giant's bath. Galveston found itself completely detached from the outside world. This city that had been in its prime and key to Texas' economy was a town reduced to unimaginable calamity and unparalleled ruin. The eighth of September not only marked the cruel demise of a glorious city in its prime, it robbed the island of its prestigious claim as a leading American harbor for shipping and immigration. In the storm's aftermath, Galveston's annihilation lead for Houston's growth. As first light broke the horizon the day after the storm, a new day indeed was dawning on Galveston. It was the rebirth of a city that would rise, though never to the prestige and power it had held only hours before the storm destroyed it. Nonetheless, the city did rise. Its weary storm survivors picked up the pieces and, with hard work and determination, the city rose again and set a new precedent on what resiliency can accomplish.

Plenty of pain—emotional, physical, psychological—was everywhere. Every man had an exceptional tale of the tragedies that befuddled him. The stress on all surviving Galvestonians was enormous. While I have no knowledge of exactly what time it was when it finally stopped raining, it must have been close to noon when the sun began to peak its way through the clouds.

Mr. Clayton took me in with his family. Because his home was on higher ground on Avenue L, damage to his home was minimal, though a few feet of water had rushed into the first floor. As a matter of fact, the Clayton's managed to take in a number of their neighbors and family members who had survived the storm. In the early afternoon, Mr. Clayton, a neighbor named Matthew Briggs, and I ventured out to rescue those needing help. It was not until we ventured further into the center of town that I realized the grander magnitude of the devastation. Every square inch of my vantage point was of total destruction in every direction I turned. Piles of debris at least ten feet high and several blocks long would be the first to overwhelm one's eye. While trying to comprehend all that comprises the mounds, one's eye would be struck by the sight of survivors staggering around in a complete daze, overrun by shock, and in desperate need of medical attention. While we wanted to disentangle the bodies of those who perished, our purpose was to help those who still had pulses rather than to worry about freeing those who had already passed away. Matthew stayed with me while Mr. Clayton went to check the status of the hospital and see if a medical station would be established for all who were injured. Sifting through a pile of lumber and glass, Matthew and I heard crying and murmurs of someone buried alive in the midst of all of the rubble. The debris that we sifted through must have been at least eight and a half feet high and thirty feet wide.

"Do you hear that?" asked Matthew with a painful expression, wiping away the sweat on his brow with the dirty white sleeve of his upper arm.

"Yes, let's try lifting this over here and see if we can get down to her."

"My friend and I can hear you, and we are working towards getting to you. It is okay for you to cry. Keep making noises so that we can follow your voice to get to you."

Queen of the Waves

The panic-stricken crying continued. It was painful work, but it was necessary work. After sifting and lifting for an hour, we finally found the woman.

"Just a few more boards and we'll have you out. What's your name, Ma'am?"

"Molly."

Matthew and I moved the last board to reveal a woman in her early twenties who had been buried alive. She had severe bruises and lacerations all over her body. Fortunately, she was trapped in an air pocket that helped keep her alive. I was concerned because she had a serious gash on the left side of her abdomen and was bleeding profusely. Matthew and I worked together to lift her out of the debris and then we gingerly placed her down in cleared area. We ripped off our shirts and pressed the dirty cotton fabric against her in an attempt to stop the bleeding from her side.

"Thank you, gentlemen, so much for helping me," whispered Molly.

Molly spoke in a quiet raspy voice. It was clear that she was suffering from severe blood loss and was growing weaker and weaker with each passing minute. Many grief stricken and traumatized people passed by, offering medical assistance, while they too were all in need of assistance themselves.

Matthew's emotions began to override his normal since of calm and restraint.

"Is anyone here that can help this poor woman? Is there a doctor?" Matthew screamed.

Determined that this woman was going to live and be a survivor, Matthew took to running all around the vicinity—climbing up and down the debris crying out for a doctor.

"He's looking for someone who can better help you."

I placed her hand in mine to comfort her and offer her some reassurance.

"How could this have happened? My family…I believe are all gone," Molly whispered looking up at me with extreme desperation in her eyes.

"But, you are alive and we are here to help you."

Molly looked back at me with glassy eyes. Her head shook a bit and then her eyes rolled upward.

"Molly. Molly. Molly! Can you hear me? Mollllyyy!"

The hand that I was holding became lifeless. At that same moment, Matthew returned without anyone to offer help. The sight of Molly's passing drove him to his knees in huge sobs.

"God, why have you forsaken us! Why did you have to take her too! She was just this innocent woman in all of this mess. Why, God? We were trying to save her! If we can't save just her, how in heaven's name are we going to be able to save ourselves from this living hell? We have churches all around. We worship you on Sunday, and now you come and destroy us! We are good people who don't deserve a reckoning! Some God you are!"

"Matthew, you are going to get yourself more hurt than you already are. You're tired and hungry. We didn't get any sleep and we are overwhelmed. Let's go find others who need our help. You can't be blaming God for this; it isn't his fault. Bad things just happen. This calamity is not God's fault."

Matthew went on screaming. He managed to climb to a high point on a mountain of debris while he continued his cursing and screaming rants towards God. It was very clear that Matthew had become insane. I climbed up the mountain of debris to get him down, but he instead punched me, called me a demon, and then shoved me off the debris pile. I then decided it was in my best interest to continue on my own through the city to look for people needing assistance. There were hundreds of people all needing help, and I did my best to continue to live in the denial that I wasn't in need of anyone's help. It was in working with others and helping them that I was able to temporarily forget about the awful circumstances I was living and all that I had lost. A sweet woman who had lost her son in the storm surge offered me one of her son's shirts. Quite moved by her gracious generosity in the midst of her loss, I decided to make my way back to St. Mary's Cathedral to find Father Kirwin and see if he was still alive. I was barely a block away from the cathedral when I came across Father Kirwin giving a final blessing to a family of nine. Father also had the expression of being sickeningly overwhelmed, but he wore it with more grace than I could.

"Woodrow, it is so good to see you. To see someone else I know is still alive; what a blessing. You survived."

"Yes, Father. It is very good to see you as well."

"How are the Sisters and the children?"

The memory of all that had happened fell over me again and I grappled once more with the horrifying images that replayed in my mind—the walls, flooring, and ceiling all collapsing in one movement; the water rushing in and everyone falling into the water; the children floundering around and the Sisters flailing in the water to stay afloat with the children; the image of a wave slamming me into the exposed stairwell as the stairs were collapsing into the storm's frothy surge, and being sucked out to sea; my frantic gasping for air and fighting to keep my head above the water before finding a door to hold

Queen of the Waves

onto. Then, the images of my finding Amelia flashed in my mind. I lost my composure and fell to my knees bawling uncontrollably.

"Oh, Father. Father Kirwin, it's not good. It was so horrible. St. Mary's…the orphanage…it is gone. It is no more. It's all gone."

I was sobbing so hard that drool came seeping out of my mouth, causing me to stutter and stumble over my words while I told Father the horrific details.

Father Kirwin's face fell from an already grim expression to a skin tone of gray from further shock. Dropping down to Woody's level, he asked, while trying to fully comprehend the extreme gravity of Woody's words, "Woodrow, what did you just say?"

"S…S…St.…St. Mary's Orphan Asylum is gone. It has been destroyed. The water and wind came in and swept everything and everyone away."

"What about the Sisters or the children? Is anyone still alive?"

"I don't know for sure; I somehow miraculously survived. But, I don't see how they could have survived. Each Sister had nine children tied to her cincture to keep the children together. The forces were working so fiercely against all of us. Father, I fear that they are all gone."

"Woodrow, you are alive, which is a blessing from God. On that blessing, let us hope that the Sisters, too, have survived. That gash on your head looks quite serious. Let's see if we can get you some medical assistance."

Father Kirwin helped me over to where a temporary clinic had been set up outside St. Mary's Cathedral. There were scores of people all having wounds cleaned and bandaged, looking for food, or searching for other loved ones. Everyone was wearing the same dismayed expression. As we walked to the cathedral, I kept surveying all of the rubble around us in disillusionment. I could not help but lock eyes with the highest point still remaining in Galveston. It was my beacon from the night that served as my compass and gave me the courage to hold on during the ferocious storm, the statue of the Blessed Mother that stood above St. Mary's Cathedral. I began to weep as I stared up at her arms reaching outward. Once again, my mind shifted back to hours before in the darkness of the storm. How the storm was raging and there she was—standing there as though she was suspended against all of the ocean's motion, a still beacon in the darkness facing the devilish sea serpent. Truly, I believed it was her grace and prayers that saved me.

Queen of the Waves

Truly, it was miraculous that Our Lady was not toppled, but still stood above the cathedral. Miraculous Mary and the cathedral bearing her name escaped almost completely unscathed. The only major damage was from the wind tearing the giant bell out of the carillon and some flooding inside the church. My mind flashed further back to the memory of when the statue was installed.

  I was roughly five years old, but I remember well when the statue of the Holy Mother was first put in place above St. Mary's Cathedral. That day left such an impression on me that it shadowed my entire life. The year was 1878. Both of my parents had passed away from the Yellow Fever epidemic that swept across Galveston. The Fever also claimed the lives of my grandparents, a couple of aunts, and my cousins. At such a young age, I was suddenly alone without a family. The Sisters took me into the orphanage, and I began the difficult task of adjusting to my new life with them and the other children. To help cheer me, Sister Agnes took me into town on one blustery day to take some bread and meat pies to the priests at St. Mary's Cathedral. On that day, there was much commotion and I was wide-eyed watching all that was taking place. The cathedral, which was badly damaged in the Civil War and in a recent storm, had been going through phases of restoration and new construction. Bishop Dubois deeply desired a new tower be added to the Church and commissioned Nicholas J. Clayton to be the architect for the new tower. In true Clayton fashion, the tower was grand. The dome-shaped tower rose from the church as though it were a beacon and what better way to illuminate the church's beacon than a prominent statue of the ultimate morning star, the Blessed Mother, the cathedral's namesake.

Mr. Clayton was not only in charge of the designs of the new dome, but he also oversaw the statue being put into place. Earlier that morning, Mr. Clayton had gone down to the wharves to find some burly men to help with hoisting the statue of Mary into place. After finding a good lot of men, he returned with a dozen strong-armed volunteers. I sat with Sister Agnes in the buggy while the men struggled to move the statue against the high southerly winds. I remember it was a very windy day. The men would pull on the ropes and the wind would blow harder against them. After several concerted efforts, most of the men were ready to give up for the day.

"Mr. Clayton. These just aren't safe conditions to be placing Our Lady atop the church. This kind of wind is going to cause the ropes to snap and the pulleys to break. Someone

Queen of the Waves

could get hurt. It is really gusting today—a little over thirty knots."

Mr. Clayton, a bit frustrated, took a deep breath and then slowly exhaled while staring at the carved stone statue of the Blessed Mother standing on the ground. As he stared at her, the wind blew through his thick curly hair, and a tremendous smile stretched across his face.

"Did you say your name is Patrick?" quizzed Mr. Clayton.

"Yes, sir."

"Well, Patrick, and fellow gentleman, we're not going to give up today on the Blessed Mother. You see, the scriptures say that the Holy Spirit always came with a great wind. Fellas, today is our day. The Holy Spirit is here to help us lift Our Lady's likeness onto her pedestal on the Church's dome. I'm certain that if we all give our best efforts in pulling her up, the Holy Spirit will help us in ascending the Blessed Mother."

The burly crew was moved by Mr. Clayton's rousing words of faith. And so, each man returned back into position and began to pull and heave on the ropes. Within minutes, it looked as if a recreation of the Assumption was taking place. Against the wind, the beautifully grand statue of Mary ascended into the sky, high above the cathedral. She was placed in position on top of the new tower without any trace of calamity. As she was put into place above the cathedral, the sun began to shine through the clouds and reflect off of the gold crown on her head. Perhaps it was coincidence, but then I'm not one who ever really believed in coincidence. It was such a glorious sight that befell us all there to witness it.

"Look at how the sun just broke through the clouds. It is as if God is smiling on us," said Sister Agnes, taking my hand and squeezing it from the excitement and awe of what she just had witnessed.

A large crowd had gathered to watch the intricately carved white statue of Mary be placed onto the specially designed tower. The exhausted crew was awestruck by how graceful the statue moved after Mr. Clayton's spirited words. Sister Agnes folded her hands and began to loudly pray the *Angelus*. Men, who interrupted their daily business and were standing around to observe the scene, removed their hats. Almost in unison, the gathered crowd bowed their heads and prayed along with Sister. Mr. Clayton then lead everyone into praying the *Our Father* and the *Hail Mary*.

There she stood! Our proud, new beacon. So majestic and royal. So strong. So bright. All in white with a carved golden crown to adorn her. It was right in that moment that I

Queen of the Waves

adopted Mary to be my new mother. The Sisters had been telling me how Mary lost her only Son. So I figured, seeing as how I had lost my mother, that she would like it if I adopted her as my mother and trusted her to mother me. I figured she was already doing a brilliant job of watching over me and praying to God for me, as I was lead from being alone to a place that bears her very name. I had found myself hardly alone, and the Sisters were taking care of me. Yes, it was right then and there at the age of five that I gave my heart to Mary and believed she would be there to help me love her Jesus and navigate through all the storms that would come into my life. Each night before going to bed, I would sneak over to the east window in the boy's dormitory to gaze at her on top the cathedral, bid her goodnight, and say my prayers to God. As a little boy, I would imagine the Holy Mother's outstretched arms were for me, and that she was reaching to hug me goodnight like my own mother used to do. I would stand there in the window and extend my arms outward to her to hug her back. I was always afraid of getting caught by one of the Sisters or other kids, but I never did get caught. And so, it became this great secret I shared just between me and the Holy Mother. I loved Sundays when the Sisters would gather us together and we would go into town to attend Mass at St.

Mary's Cathedral. As I grew older, my faith deepened not only because of those around me who were raising me, but because of how thankful I always remained for the amazing blessings that were provided for me. Even the simplest thing like a beautiful sunrise would cause me to bow my head in humble adoration of the goodness of the Lord. All the major life decisions I've had to make have been in contemplation of that glorious statue. She has been my constant compass—always pointing me and leading me to the truth of her Son and the Most High.

Where others may simply see a stone white statue above the cathedral's dome, I see so much more than that. As I sat there, with bandages being placed on my head, I could not help staring at her. This was not just a place where I went to church or just any statue. That statue, upon which I sat studying, and this church had become such a symbol of hope to me over the years, and the centerpoint of my life. Seeking consolation for my grief, I prayed:

> "Please, hear my prayer, Morning Star; help me with this nightmare that I am now living. Amidst a raging storm, I was spared. Upon seeing the image of you in the night's fury, I found the tiniest grain of hope that gave me the energy to hold on for my life when I

was ready to surrender to the storm. Please pray for me and ask the Lord to guide me to where it is that I am meant to be. For some reason, I have been spared and I don't understand why, especially when living now and seeing all of this around me is so excruciating. But, to everything there is a purpose. This, I believe, though I do not always understand what that purpose may be. Please, Blessed Mother, light my path to where the Lord wishes to lead me. Help me to be a mirror of your Son's love, light, and mercy to all of those around me who are in desperate need."

Many injured and homeless storm survivors were gathered around the perimeter of the cathedral. The church grounds were so full of wounded survivors amid the heat, humidity, and mosquitoes.

"Woodrow, please just sit and I'll get some more bandages to finish cleaning up your wounds," spoke Father Kirwin.

Suddenly being gripped with flashbacks and overcome with the passing of Amelia again, Woody reached up and grabbed hold of Father Kirwin's arm.

"Father," Woody choked and spoke as he was overcome with emotion. "Father, Amelia's dead. Her entire family was killed in the storm. Please, I beg of you, please go see her and pray over her. All of them need that. Could you, Father?"

Crying so desperately from the internal wounds and emotional scars, Woody gasped for air. Father Kirwin knelt down and looked him in the face and placed his right hand on Woody's bandaged head. He prayed over Woody and then anointed Woody's forehead.

"My dear friend, I am so truly sorry for your loss. How tragic for you to have lost your bride. Though she is with the Lord now, I know that doesn't stop the pain from this horrific tragedy. As soon as I can, I will head out and say burial prayers over them."

Father Kirwin, though stoic, was greatly troubled and exhausted by the tremendous loss that the last several hours had brought. Along with great anguish over the status of those at St. Mary's Orphan Asylum, he was further saddened by the loss of his friend's fiancée and her entire family.

Hours passed by as I sat there, working to regain my strength. All I could do was continue to stare at the Blessed Mother. A flurry of memories of life inside and around the cathedral danced before me. I loved attending Mass here. I loved the people here. They were all so good to me and were

Queen of the Waves

like family. I was supposed to have married my Amelia here. We'd already be married now if it wasn't for the storm. Of course, if it wasn't for the storm, she'd still be alive along with her family, the Sisters, the children. Everything would still be just as it was—beautiful. All the memories of all the baptisms, weddings, and funerals played around in my head. The image of the amazing blizzard in '95 and all the parishioners hurrying through the winter storm to get to Mass. The frigid morning a little over a year ago when Galveston Bay completely froze over and how Our Lady looked serene amid the frigid island sky. My mind then drifted back to the horror of just hours ago at the orphanage and I was haunted by the last images of the Sisters and the children. I wondered if any of them survived or if they were buried alive in between debris desperately needing help.

Being a person who does not like to be idle for very long, especially when a lot is on my mind, I stood up determined to make my way to find the Sisters and see if there were any survivors from the orphanage. Just as I was leaving, Father Kirwin came by with Father Sullivan.

"Father, I am going to check on the Orphanage."

"Woodrow, we found a couple of horses roaming around and gathered them. I'm not quite sure how these horses survived, but I will go with you. Father Sullivan, please take care of things here until my return. Please also let Rabbi Cohen know I have gone to check on St. Mary's Orphanage."

The men mounted the horses and rode nearly three miles to the far west side of Galveston. As they rode out, they observed the Gresham's home on Broadway. While the prominent mansion still remained in its place, mostly unharmed, Sacred Heart Church was in complete ruin across the street. In the years that followed the storm, it became neighborhood folklore that Mrs. Gresham, reaching to refasten a storm shutter, saw the collapse of the church at the height of the storm and hurried back to take refuge with her servants and children in the attic. Neither Fr. Kirwin nor Woody could fully comprehend the monumental mounds of debris or the obstacles they faced as they rode towards the orphanage.

Barely anything seemed recognizable. They passed debris piles that stood at least ten feet tall in height and were full of twisted beams, boards, siding, clothes, kitchenware, bits of furniture, fencing, glass, and bloated and bruised corpses. Upon sight of bodies amid the rubble, Father Kirwin would stop, get off his horse, say a prayer over the dead, and then carry on further through the rubble with his horse, where he would repeat the same heart-wrenching process. Occasionally,

Queen of the Waves

Father Kirwin and Woodrow passed sight of a schooner or tugboat that had been thrown inland. Even after a few hours of navigating through heavy debris and bodies, nothing could have prepared either man for the grotesquely painful sight that was in store for them once they arrived upon the orphanage's property line. Everything had been raked away. The prominent structures that were once so grand and tall on the coastal plain's horizon were gone. Shredded skeletons of what used to be a safe haven were all that remained. The sight that lay before Father Kirwin and Woody took their breath away, leading Woody to a feeling of near asphyxiation. Woody's hopes that perhaps all was not lost were dashed completely. Those wonderfully striking dormitories were swiped away along with the people he loved. The magnificent cedar trees that lined the perimeter of the property all had been uprooted and whittled apart. Debris from the buildings was strewn carelessly all over the severely gouged beach. Even the sand dunes that once stood perfectly in the foreground of the orphanage's property had been erased by the tumbling mixture of surf, sand, and debris. The beach, where the children loved to the play, had been swept away as well. A heavy foul odor that reeked of soured wood and death was starting to permeate the air.

Queen of the Waves

"Never before have I seen such destruction," I said to myself while slowly turning to take in the nightmarish panorama. I was trying to take in and comprehend the complete circle of destruction that my eyes were absorbing, as I looked from the far west and then eastward towards town. The unfathomable enormity of the destruction penetrated Father Kirwin in the same moment it hit me. We were both overcome with crushing emotion, but were in such a state of shock by what the storm did that we were left completely speechless. The images and sounds of the night before began to replay even more vividly again in my mind. Father Kirwin began moving boards around to see if there was anyone to save. He called the names of the Sisters and children in case someone might still be buried alive and needing help. Still numb, I stood frozen for awhile until noticing a seven inch piece of dingy white rope sticking out from the sand beneath a bunch of timbers. My heart quickened, as I wondered about the piece of rope. I quickly cleared the heavy timbers out of the way and pulled on the rope. Whatever it was connected to it, I could tell it seemed very heavy and was buried well beneath the sand. Frantically, I dug as fast as I could in the sand while pulling on the rope. My hands became cut from all the glass and pieces of debris that were mixed in with the sand. Increasingly, I could tell that I was coming close to what seemed to be the end of the rope. Feverishly, I worked to get to the end of the rope while calling, "Hello." My pulse quickened. At the same time, I was terrified by what I was about to unearth. I swept the last mound of sand away and pulled hard enough to reveal a drowned little body. It was sweet little Ruby Mae. I cried out immediately for Father Kirwin, who came running over. I held Ruby Mae in my arms wiping the sand off her sweet face and out of her hair. I placed her down on a board and Father Kirwin blessed her with Holy Water. Tears fell from my eyes due to the further loss I was feeling. My heart was more solemn than I knew it could be. Poor innocent Ruby Mae.

Flapping in the light wind, almost like a small flag of surrender, I noticed a small dirty white ribbon mixed in between bits of glass and a pile of boards. I felt even more raw with the loss of Ruby Mae and feared this ribbon might be the telling sign of another storm victim. Nervously, I pulled on the grimy fabric. To my surprise, it was a souvenir ribbon with a poem by Mary Hunt M'Caleb inscribed in faded gold lettering for St. Mary's Asylum Annual Picnic, dated May 5, 1877. I wiped away the muddy sand that was coating much of the poem to reveal all of the words:

These Little Ones

Queen of the Waves

Fond mothers, who hold to your bosoms tonight,
Your bright, dimpled cherubs so tenderly dear,
As you sooth the bright curls from the forehead so white.
And look in those eyes so bewitchingly clear,
Have you never thought for the little ones left
Alone in a world that is drearily cold?
Of motherly tenderness sadly bereft,
Like shivering lambs far away from the fold?
Have you never a wish in your innermost heart
To gather these little ones close to your breast;
From the wealth of your plenty to spare them a part,
That angels may whisper your name to the blest?
In robes that are costly and daintily rare,
You look on your children with motherly pride—
Womanly heart, have you nothing to spare
For the poor little ragged ones standing aside?
Standing aside in his stockingless feet,
Watching these happier children go by;
Lingering there in the dust of the street,
With a quivering lip and a tear in his eye.
But God and the angels hover near,
They look on his poverty; see all your pride—
They weigh in balance each passionate tear
That falls all undeeded so close to your side.
Then pity these lowly ones, shorn of the love
That only a mother's heart ever can give;
The cup from your hand is recorded above
In letters whose brightness forever shall live.
Uphold the brave "Sisters," who daily deny
Their hearts every tie that a woman holds dear,
With never a murmur and never a sigh,
To shelter these little ones tenderly here.
But poverty lies like a blight on their door,

Queen of the Waves

And want lays upon them her skeleton hand.
To you who are rich we appeal for the poor,
For the motherless ones of our glorious land."

The poem profoundly touched my heart, for it was written just a year before I arrived as a little boy to live at St. Mary's. It was terribly ironic for me to find the keepsake ribbon in the very spot where the main entry of the boy's dormitory stood only hours earlier. Reading the poem and seeing the date on the ribbon triggered more flashbacks, and I struggled even harder to come to terms with the imposing tragedy that enveloped me. Carefully, I folded the ribbon and put it in my pocket to keep as a memento of my life with the Sisters at St. Mary's.

"Woodrow, we're going to have to head back into town and round up those who are strong and relatively sound to start collecting all of the bodies from the rubble. So many have perished that if we don't act within the next twenty-four hours, a major epidemic may break out that could potentially kill off the rest of us. There are just so many bodies that we're going to have to start burying at sea many of those who have perished."

"Yes, Father."

"We will take Ruby Mae with us and bury her in the cemetery on our way back into town."

Queen of the Waves

Upon our journey back to St. Mary's Cathedral, we came upon the main cemetery, moved away some debris, and buried sweet little Ruby Mae in a make-shift grave. It was at Ruby Mae's gravesite that a little six-year old boy came up to us, bruised and shaken.

"Father, come here! You have to come and see this! Over there! I found them, but they are dead."

Father Kirwin, concerned by the bruises on the child and the tattered clothes he was wearing, placed his hand on the little boy's shoulder. "Son, what is it? Are you talking about your parents? Your family—they're gone."

"No, Father. I found a couple of Sisters over there. I don't know where my family is. Have you seen them?"

Startled by the double revelation as to the discovery of two nuns and the realization that this little boy was most likely a new orphan, Father Kirwin, choked back the strong emotion once more welling up inside of him. He took the little boy by the hand and asked, "Where did you find the Sisters?"

"Over there, in that pile. They have rope twisted all around them and all kinds of stuff on top of them."

"My son, what did you say your name is?"

"Jacob."

Queen of the Waves

"Jacob, I want you to stay right here with Woodrow and the horses."

Father Kirwin worked his way through the assortment of rubble to find the very location of where Jacob had found Sister Elizabeth and Sister Vincent. The site of their bodies mixed in the pile of lumber forced an immediate surge of emotion to Father Kirwin's eyes, as Father Kirwin solemnly made the Sign of the Cross. He hollered for Woody to come and help dig out the two Sisters. In working to free the Sisters from the pile, they found the bodies of eight children from St. Mary's also buried in the heap. Emily, Karen, Michael, Billy, and little Susie were still attached to Sister Elizabeth's rope. Fred, Nick, and Charlotte were not attached to any one Sister, but still had rope tied around their waists. With the bodies of all ten casualties lying free and clear of debris, both Father Kirwin and Woody knelt before them in prayer. Father Kirwin then stood up, and without saying a word, he and Woody cleared an area and dug immediate temporary graves for the ten taken souls. Woody marked the gravesites with small crosses made from lumber found in the debris pile so that their bodies could be found later for more permanent graves. It would later come to light that three boys, William Murney, Fred Madera, and Albert Campbell, were the only children to survive from

St. Mary's Orphanage in the Great Storm. All of the Sisters of Charity of the Incarnate Word perished in their noble attempt in trying to save the lives of the children. As heartbreaking as their deaths were, they died nobly fulfilling their duty in mirroring Christ's love—even in their final breaths.

Placing Jacob on the brown painted horse Woodrow had been riding, Woody walked the horse through the devastation as the men continued back into town. Along the way, Woody and Fr. Kirwin left Jacob with the Claytons for safe keeping. In the midst of gathering together volunteers and the latest news, Father Kirwin and Woodrow met up with M. P. Morrissey, steamship traffic manager, and Rabbi Henry Cohen. The two distinguished men informed Fr. Kirwin and Woody on the pertinent details of an earlier held emergency planning meeting.

"Father Kirwin, what a calamity it is that has befallen us."

"Yes, indeed."

"In the town meeting held earlier it was announced that Mayor Jones has sent word to Houston officials and to Texas Governor, Joseph Sayres, in Austin, that help desperately is needed. The initial casualty toll given to Houston officials is that five hundred have been killed. Of course, we now can clearly see that the death toll appears to be beyond two thousand lives lost.

"Father, as you have seen, the casualties are enormous. There is no way we will ever be able to bury this many people. There are great concerns among many council leaders that disease and pestilence will be on the rise if this situation isn't remedied in the immediate future," spoke Mr. Morrissey.

"Earlier today, I had the same inclination as you. Out on the west side, hundreds and hundreds of bodies are strewn about, mixed in the piles of timber and such."

"Father, there is only one thing we can do, and council and I have discussed this. We're going to have to take all of these bodies we've been gathering today and place them on barges and then sink them in the Gulf."

"I agree with you, Mr. Morrissey, and we have to do this immediately. I would say we need to be doing this no later than by sundown tomorrow."

"Yes, Father, we do. I have a group of men already going around collecting bodies and taking them to the wharf. Our hope is to ship out the deceased tomorrow night."

"I'm in the process, here with Woodrow, of gathering together a group of men as well to start collecting the dead. I'll tell the men to take the deceased to the wharf. However, we need to remember the sanctity of life and death. I'll be there with our other priests by the barges tomorrow night to say a final burial blessing. Rabbi Cohen, I expect you'll be there as well."

"Indeed, Fr. Kirwin. I will be there and will gather together other religious to help with tomorrow night's burial at sea."

"Gentlemen, I will continue in my gathering together volunteers to help. Father, if you need to get back to the cathedral to look in on things, I can take this over for you."

"Thank you, Woodrow."

In the bright moon's light, a group of thirty-five men and I sifted through the tangled heaps in search of bodies or possible survivors still clinging to life and needing medical attention. The full moon was a blessing because we had no electricity or other source to light our way through the ruins. For a moment, I heard the sound of what I thought was someone calling my name. I looked up and turned, but there was no one calling me. Instead, I saw an engorged moon shining so brilliantly behind the statue of Mary on top of the cathedral. The Holy Mother looked luminescent in the moonlight. There it was—a perfect alignment—the Queen of the Waves—so resilient and so brightly illuminated by a full moon that shone behind her as a celestial halo. I kept trying to focus on sifting through the remains, but my eyes kept being drawn upward toward the statue blazing in the night's sky. In the midst of such a hellish scene, Our Lady was a glorious sight. I felt like I was back to being that little boy in the orphanage, when I would sneak peeks at her before going to bed at night. I strangely found myself believing that the voice that had called my name was actually Our Lady and she wanted me, in the moment, to see her arms outstretched for me and everyone, and to feel the Lord's comforting beams of love and mercy. Our Lady glowed so white that I felt sure that I was experiencing some sort of apparition or miraculous phenomenon. I was so moved by the powerful moment that I just fell to my knees on top of the mountain of rubble, and clasped my hands to my heart. Some thought my mind had cracked from the day's trauma and from exhaustion. Many may say that it was nothing more than a full moon rising over a disparaged city, but there were others who also were stirred by the incredible scene. The way she glowed in the moon's perfect light, and the fact that St. Mary's Cathedral was the only building still fully intact within several blocks, inspired me and caused the grief and exhaustion to become bearable. I found myself blessed with an immediate sense of peace and a feeling that my life had been spared because I still had a purpose to fulfill for God.

We continued on the tenth day of September with sifting through debris and digging out even more bodies. The task was so overwhelming that many men were on the very literal edge of losing their minds. The entire day was nauseating. The smells and sights of thousands of decaying corpses, along with various animals and sea creatures, under a humid and torrid sun were enough to make one feel as though one would go mad from breathing in the oppressive stench that relentlessly hung in the air. In fact, while most every surviving male was working in clean up and recovery, there were some poor souls whose minds had snapped due to the hefty weight of all that they had lost and the horrors that they were witnessing. A putrid slime covered everything the sea had touched, which was most everything on the island. Men wore bandanas or rags to cover their noses in an attempt to help blot out some of the smell. Others could be seen vomiting uncontrollably from being overcome by the sour smells and overbearing heat. By late afternoon, the air was completely rancid and ripe with the odor of death and decay, as the hot summer sun broiled all that had been destroyed. The misery of those still surviving on Galveston continued to lag. It seemed the trauma wouldn't stop. The storm itself was an immeasurable agony. But, it seemed that agonies and suffering continued to increase once the storm had passed. By days end, two barges were loaded with bodies to be taken out to sea. At six o'clock in the evening, Father Kirwin and Rabbi Cohen lead a brief burial ceremony. In the lowering sunlight, the barges set out for the open waters of the Gulf. The seas were astoundingly calm compared to just twenty-four to thirty-six hours earlier. At the moment the sunlight stood halfway on the horizon of the Gulf's edge, the crew began dropping their mortal cargo into the waters, releasing the storm's casualties to their eternal rest at sea.

The sun rose the next morning, three days after the storm, to reveal a disappointing and dreadful image. Bodies were scattered everywhere on the brown sand. All of those who had perished and had been cast to sea for burial had washed back up on shore. Their bodies, decaying so severely that few individuals could be recognized, were a wretched sight. It was determined that the only way to safely dispose of so many corpses and ward off disease was to have a mass burning of the bodies in deep trenches. As one may imagine, many were overcome with exhaustion. By order of Texas Marshals, all men who did not have any serious physical limitations were ordered to begin recollecting the causalities along the beach. Many were given whiskey to help ease their emotional distress and exhaustion. It was hard enough to have gathered up so many of the deceased the first time. But now, to have to do it all over again was another added grief. The scene was such a gut-wrenching sight. Other men were ordered to begin digging trenches. Truly, the hardest part that caused the most anguish was dealing with roughly 8,000 deceased Galvestonians. Late in the evening of the eleventh of September into the early morning hours of the twelfth of September, the bodies were recollected and then set ablaze. The smell of burning human flesh mixed with the already vulgar stench, making it even harder to breathe without being overcome with the impulse of wanting to gag or vomit. The mountain ranges of debris that cascaded throughout the city were dusted lightly with soot from the large pyres, thus making Galveston hallowed ground by the way the sea's breeze carried and blew the ashes. It was all such a hellish nightmare.

We were a weary people. We were exhausted physically, emotionally drained, and spiritually strained. We still had a long arduous road of recovery before us. The road ahead would require many hours of labor and many men to get the job done, but it was a job many were willing to do. We had

Queen of the Waves

suffered a disaster beyond compare, though we were a resilient people determined to see Galveston rise again from the ruin that lay around us. We had a can-do attitude and that translated into very little whining or complaining about all we had lost. Truly, the spirit of the survivors was extraordinary. With the little that had survived the storm, citizens were sharing what they could with one another. That's not to deny that there weren't those with shady dark souls who used the heinous catastrophe as an opportunity to rob from the dead. Yes, there were those vile souls who chose to cut off the fingers of the deceased to rob them of their rings or rip a sentimental necklace off of a corpse. There were also those who chose to raid stores and loot bars. But, the Texas Marshals did a good job of keeping crimes to a minimum. Overall, the spirit of Galvestonians, these disaster survivors, was of unabashed charitable resilience.

Ships and steamers began arriving into the port three days after the storm carrying supplies not only from the U.S., but from Europe as well. Great Britain sent a ship to help move women and children out of Galveston and take them to refuge in New Orleans. Within four days after the storm, mail arrived in the city and there was the beginning of limited water service. Also, within the same week, the telegraph resumed and some banks reopened for limited business. Some streets even received back their electric lights. Surviving churches resumed with church services. On the heels of the storm, President William McKinley ordered the War Department to issue thousands of tents and thousands of rations for immediate use. As the railroads were repaired, Galveston found herself reconnected with the outside world. Help began pouring in from across the country. Even Clara Barton and the American Red Cross came to help the weary. Each day was a small step of improvement over the previous day, but the days were long and arduous.

Before long, several months had passed and town meetings were held to plan a way to prevent this tragedy from ever again happening. After much deliberation, it was voted to do the unthinkable—we voted to raise the island higher above sea level, with each family paying for the raising of their own property. We then voted to build a seawall to keep tidal surges to a minimum. Yes, we were a determined people, and the love shown to us from the outside world only helped to further ignite that pliant spark of determination in seeing Galveston persevere.

Chapter Eight

In the lantern light's glow, Marie held onto every word Woody said. Amid a raging storm, Marie found solace in learning how others had faced such intense adversity and surmounted it with formidable determination. Marie felt quite certain that she was well past the breakdown she had suffered earlier.

"Woody, I've never asked you because I didn't want to seem rude or prying, but where do you live?"

With a twinge of remorse rising up inside of him, he responded. "I live in a shelter at times, just off of Church Street. Most of the time, I stay on the beach or sit in the cemetery. I don't want to take up space that someone else with a greater need could use. Selma, she cooks for the rectory at the cathedral, always has a plate for me."

Marie didn't want to ask, but she wondered how this man, who worked so hard and who had survived so much, could be without money and homeless. Assuming Marie's thought process, Woody answered her silent question.

"I used much of the money I earned to buy markers for those in the cemetery for Amelia and her family. I regularly donated money to the rebuilding of St. Mary's Orphanage the very next year after the storm. After the first World War, I pretty much lost all that I had earned due to poor business dealings. I turned every dime I earned right back around and did something useful with it. I prayed every time that God was happy with my choices. After the Great Storm and His sparing my life, I've fully relied on Him to help me find my way to earn my next meal. When my purpose here is complete, then He'll call me home finally—this I know. The love for my Amelia has sustained me all of these years."

"I am amazed by all that you've survived and witnessed. What an outstanding gentleman you are."

"Ma'am, I didn't just witness and survive those days. With my own hands, I helped as best I could the scores of other men to cleanup this city and rebuild. As Mr. Clayton's architecture firm and health began to falter and then eventually fail, I better developed my skills as a master craftsman and carpenter. I helped rebuild houses, buildings, ships, and docks. Anywhere that I could get work, I worked as hard as I could to keep my hands busy and my mind occupied. I helped with the pouring of the sand and even with some of the laying of the beams to help raise homes when we were raising the island. All of the homes were literally raised up so that they'd be higher above sea level. That is, all of'em except the Brown house. Mrs. Brown didn't have the money for her home to be raised—so it never was—this is why you have to go down some steps to enter it."

"That is quite fascinating. I never noticed that. I had no idea," said Marie, still hanging on every word Woody had to offer. "You say that you also helped with the seawall."

"Yes, ma'am. I helped with some of the construction of the seawall. I was thrilled by the chance to be able to work on that project. It was the biggest way I could give back to the city, and I dedicated my service on the wall to the loss of my Amelia, the Sisters, and those precious children. I refused to accept one cent for the work I did on that wall…"

Woody's deeply aged sultry voice cracked. The hardness of all of the years gone by softened to a higher pitch, as tears forced their way to his eyes and began to race down his cheeks.

"I worked on that seawall so that what happened could never happen again and so that no one would have to endure that kind of loss ever again. So that no one would have to be haunted by the images I've seen—it's been a burden all of these years...." Woody's voice trailed off as he was suddenly feeling very low; all of his inner wounds were exposed completely. Tears continued to fall down his leathery face, but he worked hard to keep his emotions hidden behind the long greasy strands of grayish blonde hair.

"Ms. Marie, this is why I say for you to hold on to love. It is what saved my life. I kept living because I kept on loving Amelia, the Sisters, and those children in my heart. By and by, I should have been a dead man when that storm toppled us and took everyone I loved. But for some special reason, the good Lord saved me and kept me alive. Who knows—maybe he saved me then so that I'd be here now with you in the midst of all of this."

The rough and aged exterior of the tired old man sitting across from Marie faded, as she looked at him across the gaming table. All she saw was a man who had been carrying an enormous heartbreak. Marie's heart surged with empathy and compassion for this gentleman. She realized his rugged and scruffy exterior was due to the hard times he's endured. She saw his creases, wrinkles, and scars as badges of courage and honor. She could see fully beyond the exterior and see the

Queen of the Waves

beautiful soul that she had befriended. In hearing Woody's story, her burdens suddenly felt lighter—not gone—but just easier to bear. Wiping a few tears from her eyes, Marie smiled a sympathetic smile.

"Yes. I think maybe so. Maybe the Lord did plan for you to be here with me today. But, I believe He's saved you for something much more important than to be in yet another hurricane, only this time with a school teacher."

Finally, after a couple of hours of sitting silently, all Marie could do was internally process Woody's stories and pray for her husband's homecoming. It had been awhile since Marie heard any loud crashes, even the howling wind seemed to have quieted. The storm was subsiding. Woody felt drained. It had been many years since he had discussed the Great Storm, and even longer since he had shared his complete account of what happened to him personally in those days so very long ago. His talking about those sad days spurred many raw emotions to abruptly resurface after being buried for decades. Before him, he found all of the pain and loss tugging at him once more. The loss of Amelia felt like a re-injured sore. The wounds he thought had healed were now oozing and unscabbed. Being true to his stoic self, Woody swallowed hard and pushed the emotions back down deep inside of him.

Queen of the Waves

Marie lovingly glanced over at the picture of her Charlie and was comforted by a new surge of peace and empowerment. Woody's tale of survival inspired her and she believed that, regardless of what happened next, she would be ok and could handle whatever the future held for her.

"It definitely sounds like the storm is waning."

"Yes, ma'am. Sounds as though things are settlin down."

Just then, there was a loud frantic knock on the door.

"I wonder who is knocking," questioned Marie, as she picked up a candle and walked cautiously to the front door. The flicker of distant lightening also helped to illuminate Marie's way. Opening the door, Marie was surprised to find her soaked neighbor clinging to an equally drenched Siamese cat.

"Mrs. Winthorpe. Are you alright?"

"Marie, I was wondering if you'd mind if I could stay with you until daybreak. There's a tree that's fallen straight through on the backside of my house."

"Yes, yes of course. Please, come in out of the rain. I apologize for not being more aware. With all of the noise in the storm I had no idea something so awful happened to you. My kitchen window blew out and glass is everywhere, which gave me even more cause to hunker down as much as possible.

Please have a seat. I believe you may remember Mr. Harris. Let me get you a towel."

Marie offered Mrs. Winthorpe a chair by the gaming table next to Woodrow. Mrs. Winthorpe was thought by many to be the Grand Dame of the neighborhood. She, in her sixty years of life, was always available to provide guidance to all of her neighbors, regardless of whether the advice was sought or not.

"I thought you'd like a towel to help you dry off from the rain."

"Oh thank you, my dear."

Mrs. Winthorpe, looking quite frazzled, but trying to remain polite, nervously smiled at Woodrow as she took her seat. "Yes, I remember you; we've met on many occasions."

Woody just nodded back expressionlessly at Mrs. Winthorpe.

"Mrs. Winthorpe, you should have sought refuge here sooner."

"I would have, my dear, but that storm was blowing things around so. I thought it best to lay low until things calmed down for good. The storm fooled me a bit earlier. Right when I thought we were done, we suddenly got the another blast. No, I just stayed in place. I didn't want to get out of the house only to have something fall on me or pierce right through me on my way to seek refuge."

"Very true, Mrs. Winthorpe. As far as I can tell, I've lost my kitchen window and some windows upstairs. Sadly, I think we also lost the magnolia tree in the backyard. But, I'll be able to tell more in the morning light. I'm thankful Mr. Harris came by to warn about this storm. I was in a deep sleep this morning, and to my surprise it was storming so when I awoke. If it hadn't been for Mr. Harris knocking on my front door to warn me, I would not have known what was going on outside. During the storm, Mr. Harris was telling me about the 1900 storm from which he survived, but so very many perished."

Politely smiling, but still looking nervous from the storm that had attacked her house, Mrs. Winthorpe added, "Oh, indeed. Mr. Harris, I have seen you around and at the cathedral, but I never knew you are a survivor of that legendary storm. Bless your heart. Then, I'm sure this squall, as dreadful as it is, was nothing from what you experienced previously."

"No, ma'am—this was a pretty good squall. Perhaps like the one in 1915."

"Indeed, it was. It just came up so suddenly with no warning. On the radio this morning, there was no mention of anything like this. My poor husband is still, at this late hour, stuck at the factory in all of this." Mrs. Winthorpe wiped her brow with her forehead as beads of perspiration and anxiety culminated on her heavy brow.

Wearing a concerned expression, Marie nodded her head in full agreement, "Yes, there was no warning at all. Barely a mention was made on the radio. This is all very peculiar. I cannot imagine why there hasn't been any real acknowledgement of this powerful storm we've just experienced."

"Well, my dear, I believe it's because we're at war. Plain and simple. With all these drills we've suffered through these past couple of years and the alerts of Germans out in the Gulf right off our coast. My husband, Bill, has talked about those U-boats skulking around off our shores. They could not acknowledge on radio how bad things are because that would be an open invitation to attack us," said Mrs. Winthorpe in a most austere tone.

"Yes, I suppose you're right. These are very difficult times with little news being shared all the way around," said Marie.

Still delicately wiping her brow, Mrs. Winthorpe chimed, "Say, in the height of the storm, did either of you happen to hear a sound that sounded like a plane at times?"

Queen of the Waves

Marie was stunned, as she thought the noise may have been her overactive imagination despite Woody's acknowledgement of hearing the same sounds. "Yes! Indeed, I did. I was having an anxiety attack because I just knew that we were about to be attacked by the Germans. And, I'm still not certain that we aren't about to be."

As the two ladies exchanged commentary on what they heard and how scared and vulnerable they felt, Woodrow sat at the gaming table in the lantern light watching the two ladies. He quietly savored not being alone. From Marie's frequent visits to the cemetery to clean graves, through the course of this squall, and through the evening with Mrs. Winthorpe, he realized that real companionship was something he'd been without for decades. He was thankful to God and humbled for not only the gift of the new friendship he had in Mrs. Marie Covington, but in making it through another historical storm.

The dawning of July 28, revealed the night's secrets. Galveston had been ravaged by a mighty hurricane, though the storm's victims didn't yet know they were officially hit by a hurricane. It would be weeks until the National Weather Service could officially release notice that the storm indeed was a hurricane and decades until all of the classified documentation regarding the storm would be declassified for the public to learn the complete account of the storm's history. Though small in comparison to the Great Storm of 1900 or even the storm of 1915, this hurricane caught most every citizen by surprise, and caused substantial damage, at a most vulnerable time. The small towns dotting the southeast Texas coast housed many factories and refineries that produced the key commodities of fuel, steel, and aluminum needed for America's war effort. Most of the factories and refineries experienced extensive damage, while some were completely destroyed. Trees were strewn about the city. Many homes and businesses had busted windows, ripped off roofs, and snapped power lines. In all, twenty people were killed and thousands were made homeless. Adding to the anxiety, shelters for storm victims were discouraged due to a Polio outbreak. While physical damage was immediately evident upon the hurricane's powerful passing, it would be years before the storm's true significance would be fully realized. The 1943 hurricane went down in history for reasons having little to do with the storm's fierceness, as it set a precedent in censorship by the United States military and government during a state of war. It was also the first hurricane in which an Air Force pilot deliberately flew directly into a hurricane to monitor its position and strength, setting a precedent for what would be developed over time into a complete air reconnaissance program for the National Oceanic and Atmospheric Administration to monitor hurricanes in the Gulf of Mexico and Atlantic basin.

Marie was pleased to confirm in the morning light that her house suffered minimal damage. The magnolia tree in the backyard had blown over after knocking out her kitchen windows. Her giant tree was a complete loss. The windows in the master bedroom and guestroom had all been shattered by the fierce winds. As Marie began cleaning up the snapped limbs, roof shingles, and broken glass in her yard, she was thankful that her house wasn't smashed like Mrs. Winthorpe's or some other homes down the street. Four houses down, Marie carefully watched as a military chaplain arrived at the McKellan's home to deliver the news that Steve McKellan would not be coming home alive from the war, and that Mrs. McKellan would have to face raising their two little boys on her own. Marie's mind jolted back, almost as a defense mechanism, in fancying Woody's words about the 1900 storm and living for love. These thoughts caused Marie's apprehension to once again release and another surge of empowerment circulated through her. As she contemplated Woody's words about a broken world, she found comfort in believing that she would be able to survive all of the brokenness the world was presenting her. She made a commitment to herself as she slowly turned a complete circle in her yard, while taking in all of the chaos around her, that she was going to start living more deliberately out of love. After all, in one single stroke, all that is precious can be torn away by a sudden swift change in the winds of life.

"Good afternoon, Ma'am!"

"Why Woody, you startled me! I didn't expect to see you back so soon. I was just taking in all of the damage around me. You said you'd be going to see St. Mary's Cathedral to see if Mary was still standing atop the Church."

"Yes'em. She's still there. I came back to bring you these as a token of saying thank you for letting me take refuge in your home during the storm. Please take them as a sign of friendship."

A cheerful smile spread across Marie's face. "My goodness, what a beautiful basket of strawberry plants. Where ever did you find such pretty plants?"

"Mr. Blalock at the nursery lets me sift through his trash for any herbs or produce that I might want. Much of the nursery was damaged in yesterday's storm. He said I could have these since he was going to throw them out. I wanted you to have these strawberry plants as my gift to you as a symbol of victory."

Marie graciously accepted the basket of strawberry plants and motioned for Woody to have a seat on her front porch. Woody, with his age truly showing, slowly followed her with a slight limp. Woody sat down on the white wooden bench on Marie's front porch. Marie sat down across from Woody in the white wicker rocking chair.

"You see, after the 1900 Storm, Clara Barton came in with the American Red Cross, and as part of Galveston's recovery effort the next year, she helped develop strawberry farms just north of here. Those strawberries became a cash crop that helped this area's local economy. I worked for awhile on a strawberry farm in Pasadena. Pasadena, indeed. We grew the strawberries so well that people thought they were just as good as the ones from California. So, that little development just to the north of here was named Pasadena after the city in California—and that's all a direct result of that unprecedented Great Storm. Those strawberries were such a cash crop for this area that they helped many survivors to begin rebuilding their lives."

"Woody, that's remarkable. I had no idea strawberries could be grown this far south. Your tidbits of history fascinate me," cordially smiled Marie, intrigued by Woody's story. "I will add these plants appropriately to my victory garden in the back, as in your story, these will serve to be a reminder to me of perpetual hope."

By nightfall the next day, Marie had done just as she said she would. In the midst of cucumbers, green beans, okra, tomatoes, sweet peppers, and cantaloupes, Marie carefully planted the precious strawberry plants in her garden. She knew, as she planted each green plant and admired the dainty white flowers, that a new side of her also was taking root. She couldn't wait to write all of this newly found enlightenment and gained historical knowledge in a letter to Charlie.

Chapter Nine

The sultry summer sun surrendered itself to the late seasonal changes of September. A new school year was in full swing. Marie continued to visit the cemetery every Saturday, where she visited Woody. She used the time to bring him extra food or clothing, just as she did shortly after meeting him. World War II was still raging. Though Marie poured out as many letters to Charlie as fast as she could write them, news from Charlie was very slow until this day. Today, the postman delivered a small bundle of letters from Charlie. There were thirteen letters all dated with various dates throughout the summer. While Marie's mind started to fear the worst upon receipt of the bundle of letters, she held onto the hope he would be home soon, and that this bundle was just a fluke. Again, she found the wisdom from Woody's stories to be true—by living in love, you find peace within yourself. She decided to hold onto that peace and to seize this day that brought her words

Queen of the Waves

from her Beloved. Thus, it was a very special day. It was a moment to celebrate and cherish after not hearing from him for so very long. Marie packed a picnic lunch and planned to read her Charlie's words on the beach and then pen an immediate response.

The day was an absolute pristine day. The wind was slight and the surf was quite mild. Stretched out on a sunflower colored tablecloth with the sun at her back, munching on a strawberry, Marie closed her eyes and imagined Charlie sitting across from her. It had been so long since she saw him in person. She conjured the image of her husband into her mind. To her surprise, his laugh was the first thing that came back to her; it was almost as if she could hear him amid the sea's breeze. She then recalled his golden hair, his gentle blue eyes, and that smile. He had the brightest smile she knew in anyone, and he knew how to use it to keep her from getting too mad at him sometimes. She recalled his shoulders and how sturdy they were and how good he was with crafting and building things with his hands. She missed how perfectly her hand fit into his hand. Her heart pounded with joy, as Charlie was before her in memory. An overwhelming smile grew across Marie's face and her heart beamed. Gingerly, she picked up the thirteen letters and read each one. As the hours passed, she read how her

Queen of the Waves

Charlie loved her and how desperately he wanted to come home. She learned about the brutal conditions and how many in his troop had been killed in a skirmish. Between the lines, she could tell how lonely he was and the trouble that was ever-present around him.

As Marie finished reading the last letter, she gently ran her fingers across the writing, hoping she would somehow be able to feel him or touch his heart. Marie's eyes welled with salty emotion. Slowly, she closed her tearful eyes and reached for the locket she was wearing. Clutching the round gold locket with an engraved cross resembling a compass, she remembered Charlie giving her the locket the first night in their new home in Galveston. The locket was a most precious treasure, and it meant even more now that Charlie was somewhere in the midst of a different type of storm. Affectionately, she opened the locket to read the words he had imprinted, "Always…More Than Words." The message was to remind her that he would always love her more than words could ever convey. She cherished that reminder and closed her eyes to remember how much she loved wrapping her arms around him and how much she missed when they would just hold each other. As the sun began to set, Marie prayed for Charlie's safety, and then gathered up her basket. Marie noted how dazzling the sky

Queen of the Waves

looked with its brilliant hues of peach and pink clouds while walking home. Approaching her gate, she noticed a shadowy figure sitting on her front porch. Immediately, Marie thought Woody had come to see her and to share with her some news about St. Mary's or share another tale of island folklore. The oak tree's far reaching arms shadowed the porch, making it hard to see. Marie's mind curiously racing, her thoughts jumped from the visitor not being Woody to it being Mr. Winthorpe or one of the other neighbors. Perhaps, it could be Bootsie or Moxie with some kind of invitation. As she opened the gate, she could see that the dark silhouette was a military figure. A jolt stronger than the hottest lightning shot through Marie, as she suddenly believed her worst nightmare was coming true. Her Charlie was dead. She feared her Charlie had breathed his last breath. She believed the one waiting for her on the porch was someone sent to notify her that her husband indeed had been killed. Her knees wobbled and her lips quivered as she fought hard to control her emotions. A huge knot formed in her throat that made her feel as though she could not breathe. For a moment, she felt like she might have a seizure or faint. Marie labored to catch her breath and pulled herself together. She hesitantly crept up the pathway, terrified to hear the words she knew to be inevitable. The figure saw her and slowly stood up.

"Oh God in heaven, please give me strength. Mary, Queen of the Waves, please pray for me in this very moment," Marie whispered to herself, as she meekly continued up her walkway. The dark figure slowly walked across the porch and arrived at the top of the porch steps. After a hesitant pause, the shadow stepped further into the light and began to descend the steps.

"Marie."

The wind was completely knocked out of Marie. All circuits in her nervous system were immediately overloaded. The basket Marie was carrying from the beach dropped out of her hand and hit the ground. Pages from all of Charlie's letters took flight in the evening breeze and fluttered across the front lawn. Except for the tears falling from her face uncontrollably, Marie was paralyzed. She struggled to get her tongue and lips to move in perfect sequence so that she could answer the dark figure. After a long pause, Marie found the composure to utter a single syllable.

"Yes."

Marie bolted for the steps in almost one movement. The figure, out of the darkness, was there to meet her and snatch her up at the bottom step. Tears flooded Marie's eyes. She gushed with deep emotion, as an electric smile seized her face.

"Charlie! I can't believe it's you. You've come home to me," wailed Marie, as she continued to cry, kiss him, and hold him close to her.

"I'm home, sweetheart. I'm home!" Charlie exclaimed, as he continued to kiss her and hold her.

Charlie and Marie held onto each other tightly. Quite dismayed and completely choked up, Marie struggled to speak.

"I can't believe you are here to welcome me home. It was supposed to be the other way around!"

"It's okay, Bunny," said Charlie, still cradling Marie in his arms while gently gliding his hands up and down her back, and repeatedly kissing her on the lips, forehead, and cheek.

Taking a hold of his hand, Marie stepped back. "Are you okay? I didn't expect you. I didn't receive any notice you were coming home. Are you alright?"

"I'm fine. That is I'm fine now. I was shot in the leg and neck in a mild combat, busted a few ribs, and my right hip. I finally healed enough to travel and so I've been sent home. I'll be just fine."

Marie cried more tears upon hearing Charlie say he had been shot. She squeezed his hand and reached to embrace him again, but then hesitated. "I want to hold you, but I don't want to hurt you."

Charlie, completely unable to take his eyes off of his bride in the moon's gaze, smiled broadly at Marie. As Marie continued to talk, her exact words faded a bit from Charlie's mind. Charlie too was feeling quite overwhelmed—bombarded by a flood of emotions of finally being home with his delightful bride. Constantly in his heart and mind, as he fought in battles across France, was Marie. Charlie had serious doubts as to whether he ever would make it back home to her. He adored her—he knew that upon first meeting her. Now that she was standing before him, he was taken aback by how much more he adored her. As Marie stood there in the moonlight at the bottom of the porch steps, she appeared to him as an immaculate angel. He could not help the fascination that fell upon him while marveling at how the moonlight danced upon her hair and face, and how she looked so glorious. All Charlie could do was smile broadly at Marie and gently pull her back towards him.

"You could never hurt me. I'm going to be just fine. Come here and let's go inside. It is so good to be home."

They exchanged a passionate embrace and then went inside their home. While Charlie told her the details of where

Queen of the Waves

he was stationed, the people he met, and stories about the war, Marie prepared, as best as she could, a feast for the both of them. She worked to scrounge up as many of Charlie's favorites as she could: fried chicken, tomato and cucumber salad, and green beans. Using the biscuits leftover from the morning and some strawberries from the plants she had planted from Woody months earlier, she served a variation of strawberry shortcake for dessert. Charlie savored every morsel on his plate, but relished more being home with Marie. They stayed up until almost dawn swapping stories of all they had experienced in their time apart. It was not until five in the morning when Marie finally went to bed.

"I'm going to set the alarm clock for eight so that we can get up and get to Sunday Mass on time. There's someone I want you to meet...." Marie's voice fell abruptly to a whisper. Charlie had fallen sound asleep. Still overcome with the wonderment that he was safely home and asleep beside her in their bed, Marie reached and pulled the bed sheet and light blanket a little further over Charlie. Tenderly, she kissed him on the forehead and rested her head for a moment against his head. She then curled up next to him, careful to not wake him. Misty-eyed with joy, Marie fell asleep watching Charlie slumber.

Queen of the Waves

Chapter Ten

The weeks flew by faster than Marie could count with Charlie home. The return to living a married life under the same roof came quite easily for Marie and Charlie, though Charlie was still working through some internal struggles from having been in war and witnessing so much horror. Together, they fixed up the house and became quite active at St. Mary's Cathedral. Charlie, upon receiving a complete military discharge, was back to building business connections. Through Marie, Charlie befriended Woody, and on several occasions offered him shelter, including the offer to live with them. Woody always refused help. Even in the midst of the heavy storms that pounded Galveston and spawned a deadly tornado the second week of November, Woody weathered things on his own terms. Just as Marie had learned, Charlie learned that Woody was a man with an amazing spirit, but he certainly had a mind of his own.

Queen of the Waves

"Charlie, I'm thinking we should invite Woody over for Christmas dinner. Maybe we could have him over first for a Sunday dinner and to help us decorate the Christmas tree. I think he might enjoy that."

"That sounds like a lovely idea. We should."

"Good. I'm so glad you agree. How about we ask him tomorrow when we go to the cemetery? I have some poinsettias I would like to take for the Sisters and children."

The Covingtons had a tremendous amount to be thankful for and to celebrate. Marie could not wait to meet up with Woody and share the tidings of joy and thankfulness that hallmark the season. With wild excitement, Marie could not wait for the next day to come, to extend their Christmas invitation to their dear friend. The next morning, she could not get to the cemetery fast enough. She hurried through the cemetery's wrought iron gate, as Charlie opened it. They proceeded to the far back corner where Amelia Franco and the others from the Great Storm were buried. Approaching the small gate that used to be hidden by a wall of oleanders, Marie could see Woody propped up against Amelia's headstone. The gate loudly clanged and squealed as Charlie and Marie entered the special area. The air was moist and cold. The trees looked as though they were on fire with their bright reds, oranges, and yellow leaves.

"Oh, he must be asleep. I bet he was awake all night long. Woody, it's me and I've brought Charlie...Woody...."

Marie gently reached for his arm to shake him, but there was no warmth to him. She nudged him again. There was no response. Marie took a nervous tone.

"Woody...Woody...Charlie, something is wrong."

Charlie knelt down and felt Woody's arm and pulse.

"Honey, he's gone," Charlie softly said, looking into Marie's concerned eyes.

"No, he can't be! He's survived everything it seems. He can't die. He...he can't be," softly cried Marie.

"Sweetheart, your friend has passed from living a long and remarkable life," said Charlie in a most consoling tone. "And, look at this—I believe this is what caused Mr. Harris's death."

Marie jumped back out of fright. To the side of Amelia Franco's headstone was a four-foot-long rattle snake that had been decapitated.

"My gosh, he was killed by the snake. It poisoned him. Look at his arm here. Yes, you can see the puncture marks from the bite."

"But, it looks like Mr. Harris got the last laugh and beheaded the snake before passing," Charlie said while maneuvering the snake around with a large sturdy stick.

"I hope there aren't any other snakes around here."

Charlie cautiously looked around for a bit. "No, everything looks okay."

Moved with grief over the sudden loss of her friend, Marie continued kneeling beside Woody. She noticed Woody died holding an old worn book in his hands. Marie reached to take the book from his grasp and discovered it was his Bible bookmarked with an antiqued white ribbon. Upon closer examination, she discovered the white ribbon was inscribed with a faded poem. The gold lettering for the poem was barely visible. With the letters that were still somewhat legible, she could make out that the poem was entitled "These Little Ones." Marie noticed the passage circled on the open page of the Bible was from the Book of Revelation:

> A great sign appeared in the sky, a woman clothed with the sun, with the moon under her feet, and on her head a crown of twelve stars…Then another sign appeared in the sky; it was a huge red dragon, with seven heads and ten horns, and on its heads were seven diadems…The serpent, however, spewed a torrent of water out of his mouth after the women to sweep her away with the current. But the earth helped the woman and opened its mouth and

Queen of the Waves

swallowed the flood that the dragon spewed out of its mouth. Then the dragon became angry with the woman and went off to wage war against the rest of her offspring, those who keep God's commandments and bear witness to Jesus ...

Marie was humbled and taken aback by the passage and immediately understood why the passage appeared to mean so much to Woody, especially upon his least breath and the peculiar circumstances that caused his death.

"Charlie, we need to get a priest." Tears slipped past Marie's eyes. She slowly placed her hand back on Woodrow's arm, unable to believe that this remarkable life had been extinguished.

"This is where I met you. I was in so much pain and scared about so very much. You came through that gate, walked into my life, and taught me so much about this town's history, about the incredible lives of the people who rest in peace here. You taught me the importance of being resilient, and holding on to faith, hope, and love amid the blackest darkness. You reminded me of how love is the most important thing in this world. Most importantly, you taught me how to dig deep and weather the storm. We became friends; you helped as I bared my grief and held onto my hope of welcoming my Charlie home—and he came home. You both became friends too, and now...I'm so sorry you're gone. But, so blessed by the light you shined into my life."

Tearfully, Marie raised her right thumb and made the Sign of the Cross on Woodrow Harris's forehead.

"Rest in peace, Mr. Harris. I pray that you are now happily in heaven with your Amelia and all of those you so dearly loved."

"Sweetheart, let's go notify Father Carmichael of Woody's passing and get him a final blessing."

Crying, Marie nodded her head and took Charlie's hand. Charlie pulled her close, sympathizing with her loss.

"Charlie."

"Yes, my love."

"I want us to provide Mr. Harris with a proper funeral at the cathedral. He deserves that after all he's survived and sacrificed. He deserves an honorable funeral because he was a most honorable man."

"Yes, sweetheart, we'll see that he is given a proper tribute."

The clouds, as thick as unprocessed cotton, filled the cold early winter air. The first impressionable cold front of the season had arrived. A squadron of pelicans flew overhead coincidentally forming a formation reminiscent of a military air salute. The carillon bells sounded a death knoll, as the clock chimed ten in the morning. Mourners took their seats inside St. Mary's Cathedral on this somber eighth day of December. Well beneath the statue of Mary, Star of the Sea, in front of the ornate white marble altar railing, was Woody in a simple pine coffin. The cathedral was overloaded with mourners and well wishers who came to the funeral Mass to celebrate the beautiful and tragic life of Mr. Woodrow James Harris. There were few dry eyes in the Church. People from all over Galveston came to extend their respect to this extraordinary Great Storm survivor, who had transcended tragedy on so many occasions by working and giving unselfishly to meet the needs of others.

At noon, with the sun piercing through the heavy clouds to offer mourners some warmth, the white statue of Mary shone so purely in the sun's light. Woodrow Harris was laid to rest alongside the grave of Amelia Franco. After a little over four decades since the 1900 Storm, he finally was at peace with his Beloved. Woody had been called home. Marie walked up to place a final red rose upon Woody's coffin in the freshly dug grave. This friend that she accidentally encountered because of her curiosity of some hidden gravestones had changed her life forever. As the rose slipped from her fingers, she knew that the course of her life had been permanently altered. She vowed

Queen of the Waves

once more to herself to live her life more purposefully with the same unselfish zeal and love that Mr. Harris lived his life. As a teacher, she felt in her heart that Woody's death marked the passing of a torch. It was now Marie's turn to emblazon new generations with the light of not only Galveston's legacies and rich history, but the notion that every life has a special purpose for this world. Truly, in the end, love never fails; it ultimately conquers the darkest of evils.

Queen of the Waves

Chapter Eleven

Deep azure skies glowed over Galveston on this glorious Friday in May. Green lush trees swayed in the cool breeze. Planter boxes lining the harbor decks teemed with tulips, roses, and Gerber daisies. The island was awash with vivid color, a refreshing change from the monochromatic rubble that surrounded the area months earlier. It has been a year and eight months since the mirror image of the Great Storm came calling to Galveston's shores. Unlike the Great Storm of 1900, this storm had a name, and it was named Ike.

Large round tables draped with white linen tablecloths and adorned with pink oleander centerpieces lined Pier 21, alongside the Tall Ship Elissa. Women in sundresses and gentlemen in refined casual wear luncheoned on a succulent seafood buffet. Slightly before one in the afternoon, a tall slender woman in her middle sixties with long brown hair and

Queen of the Waves

deep brown eyes, wearing a soft yellow dress approached the podium and smiled exuberantly at the seated audience.

"Hello, everyone. Thank you for coming today to support Galveston's Historical Foundation and to celebrate this year's recipient of Galveston's Steel Oleander Award. For those of you who don't know me, I am Olivia Covington. I am here today to present this year's award to my mother, Marie Covington. As most of you know, for over sixty years my mother has worked tirelessly as a volunteer in the perpetual beautification of our dear city and in teaching the incredible history of all this city has endured and overcome. Marie Covington also has devoted her life in working with St. Mary's Cathedral Basilica, St. Patrick's Catholic Church, Sacred Heart Catholic Church, with the Galveston Historical Foundation, Catholic Charities, and the American Red Cross. My mother has worked hard to ensure that, regardless of which storm may blow into town, the roots of Galveston's youth and the surrounding community may continue to hold steadfast.

In the aftermath of this terrible monster named Hurricane Ike, I, along with all of you, toast my mother, Marie Covington, for the beacon she has been in radiating Galveston's legendary resilience. Mother, while she appears so meek and mild, is a courageous woman with a steel resolve.

Queen of the Waves

While my father was at war, mother faced the Gulf Coastal front on her own. Mother used to tell us about how, during the 1943 hurricane, she heard sounds similar to a plane and just knew Galveston was on the brink of being attacked and invaded. What my mother and others actually heard was a flight that British Colonel Joseph Duckworth and Lt. Colonel Ralph O'Hair took from Bryan Field directly into the hurricane to examine the storm's strength, intensity, and track. Who would have ever guessed that in the midst of that powerful hurricane, with possible German U-boats offshore, that my mother was hearing the sounds of the first-ever Air Force reconnaissance flight that would provide the initial model for the way future hurricanes would be studied and monitored? This Steel Oleander gave witness and survived a hurricane that was kept a complete secret by the U.S. Government to maintain National Security on our shores during World War II.

My mother has handed down her own legendary stories to the children who have had the good fortune of being in her classroom. But, the truth is that my mother would tell you that her inspiration came from a simple man with an extraordinary story whom she met in the cemetery one day in early July 1943. My father was away at war and she was petrified that she'd never see him again—that he'd be lost to the storm that

Queen of the Waves

had seized the world at that time, and that America, too, would be lost. But, over the course of several weeks, this stranger, Mr. Woodrow Harris, revealed to my mother that he was a survivor of the Great Storm of 1900. He shared in detail how he had watched most everyone he cherished from St. Mary's Orphanage falter in the swift tide and then found he also had lost this bride to be on what was suppose to have been their wedding day. Mr. Harris shared with my mother the stories of how, despite the seemingly insurmountable obstacles and catastrophic losses, he and the remaining survivors that very next day after the Great Storm wiped their tears and got to work. This city had to survive because they were not only still living, but they were now living for those who had perished. From the lessons Woody, as he was called, shared with my mother, we on the Texas Gulf Coast are resilient. While we are thankful for those who offer their help, we do not sit around waiting for someone to save us. Instead, we bounce back stronger and eager to help each other overcome whatever tragedy is thrown our way. We have an indelible spirit and have proven this throughout our history, and we've just shown the world our impeccable buoyancy again in the face of Hurricane Ike. Yes, the economy is sour and there's a perfect political storm brewing in the world; but, as we've shown, we are rebuilding. We are rising again. Resiliency is a life lesson that needs to be shared and mirrored. And, Mr. Harris's deeper lesson is even truer: The only thing that can sustain you in this world is love. If you do not have love in your heart and aren't living out that love to others, then obstacles will always be impossible to overcome. It is because of Mr. Harris sharing his story, Galveston's story, that my parents became so inspired that they adopted me from St. Mary's Orphanage in 1950. My brother, Christopher, and my sister, Mary Alice, became part of our family when they were both adopted from St. Mary's in 1953, just before the doors were permanently closed and the building torn down. With amazing grace, my mother has been a fine fixture here in Galveston. Without further ado, I'd like to present this year's Steel Oleander Award to my mother, a true beacon, Marie Covington."

Slowed by age, Marie unsteadily stood up with the help of her son, Christopher. Charlie, beaming with pride, shakily kissed his bride on the cheek. Both moving slowly, Charlie walked Marie to the stage. Amid a standing ovation, Olivia, Christopher, and Mary Alice helped their parents up the steps of the stage for Marie to receive her award. Wearing a vibrant blue dress and glorious smile, Marie was thrilled and beaming. Her white hair was cut short just above the top of her shoulders and her cheery face bore a multitude of creases. In the moment while everyone reclaimed their seats, Marie turned her head and gazed at her beloved Charlie. Her mind flashed back to the day he came home from the war and she thought about how that was her proudest moment—even more momentous than the blessed adoptions or the one she was currently living. With all of the years that had passed, Marie still deeply loved this man and she rejoiced for how her living in the love for this man had saved her sanity so many times. Marie's misty eyes scanned back ahead of her and over the crowd to see the magnificent ivory statue of Mary atop the Basilica floating above the skyline in the afternoon sun. Internally, Marie said a quick, silent prayer of thanksgiving for the Star of Sea being there all of these years as a reminder of perpetual hope when hope seemed so fleeting.

As is typical in the evening, a tender wind picked up as the sun prepared to set in the western sky. Marie, holding onto her cane, struggled to kneel down at Woodrow's grave. Seeing her mother's struggle, Olivia rushed to help her mother.

"What an amazing day today was, to be given the Steel Oleander Award," beamed Marie, talking to the white marble tombstone. "I want you to have this because it has been your legacy that I've been passing on all these years."

Queen of the Waves

Marie made the Sign of the Cross, bowed her head, said a prayer, and then placed the cut crystal award on Woody's marker along with half of the red roses from the bouquet she received. Marie struggled to get up, took a few steps over, and placed the remaining six red roses on Amelia Franco's grave. Marie then turned and looked back at Woody's grave and smiled.

Queen of the Waves

Epilogue

Forces are constantly in motion, shaping outcomes. In finishing this story, the original ending was altered due to Hurricane Ike slamming into Galveston on September 12, 2008, before the author's very eyes. Hurricane Ike was, in the truest essence, an exact mirror image of the infamous Great Storm. Thanks to the innovation and determination of Galveston's predecessors over a century ago, there was a seawall to provide some protection from a repeated horrific fate—though Ike had little trouble climbing the seawall to deliver destruction to thousands of people, and seriously harming many of Galveston's historical treasures. Many of the historical homes and buildings in Galveston that are mentioned in this story were badly damaged, especially St. Mary's Cathedral Basilica. Tragically, St. Mary's entire sanctuary was seriously injured by the eight feet of water that poured into the church from Hurricane Ike's initial storm surge. An important landmark of Texas history, St. Mary's Cathedral Basilica is still closed for repairs and restoration. A large percentage of

Queen of the Waves

proceeds from this book will be contributed to the St. Mary's Cathedral Basilica Restoration Fund so that her remarkable legacy and example may continue to shine for future generations. While St. Mary's sanctuary took a painful hit, the legendary statue of Mary was unscathed by Ike and still stands prominently in place amid Galveston's skyline. It truly has been inspirational to witness Galveston's resilient spirit shine forth and the city resurrect itself once more.

Queen of the Waves, may you continue to be a beacon of perpetual hope.

Made in the USA
Charleston, SC
03 January 2013